SHERLOCK HOLMES IN CANTERBURY

MILES ELWARD

WYNNE HOWARD
Publishing

First Published May 1995
by
Wynne Howard Publishing
10 Betula Close
Kenley
CR8 5ET

ISBN 0 9525571 0 X

Copyright Wynne Howard Publishing

Sherlock Holmes in Canterbury

Contents

The Missing Cleric...........................page 1
The Sunleys of Canterbury ....page 27
The Ball of Twine ....page 51

To My Beloved
Danielle Claire
and
Benjamin David

Note: This book has sought to achieve historical accuracy, but the main locations of each story are, with the exception of the most obvious landmarks, inventions and not existing sites.

The Missing Cleric

"No, I am sorry to disappoint you Watson, but I am still not interested," ejaculated Holmes, holding up his hand. "For the last five mornings and on at least three evenings, you have attempted to regale me with the latest reports of this wretched case. I refuse to listen."

He helped himself to another cup of coffee and returned to perusing the agony columns of the various morning papers. Occasionally he would circle an entry in red pencil and emit a grunt of surprise or satisfaction in a manner designed to show that he was paying me no attention whatsoever.

Although Holmes could, as a man of varied interests, talk knowledgeably on such matters as sixteenth century ecclesiastical architecture, he seemed to lack any aptitude for the benefits offered by organised religion. His own moral principles may have been as rigid and unwaveringly held as those of an anglican bishop, but he would regularly mock the pompous vanities of the zealots from both evangelical and catholic wings of the church. As a result he considered the fall from grace of a well-regarded clergyman as of little interest.

For my part, however, I was enjoying the generous coverage devoted to the affair of the "adulterous anglo-catholic" as it had become known. According to the reports a respected, and married, anglo-catholic clergyman, whose church stood in the very shadow of Canterbury Cathedral, had run off with a young milkmaid from a farm in the surrounding countryside. It was assumed that they had fled across the Channel to France to live in sinful union. Doubtful sightings of the couple were reported from Amiens, Paris and, most improbably, Marseille.

At eleven o'clock Mrs. Hudson brought up the second post and Holmes fell on it with the energy of a man desperate for a new challenge, but as he opened the first letter he let out a loud groan. "This is impossible Watson. Who are these fools? Do they take me for a moral crusader, or a member of a temperance league?"

I looked up in amazement at this outburst and Holmes seeing my curiosity thrust the letter into my hand. It read:

From the Dean of Canterbury Cathedral

I will call on you at eleven o'clock this morning to consult you on the matter of the disappearance of the Revd. Russell.

Yours etc.

As I read, the bell sounded below and Holmes groaned again. Heavy footsteps mounted the stairs and Holmes and I received, what can only be described as a clerical visitation. The Dean himself strode into the room, his black top hat almost brushing the door frame, and his bulky figure crammed into black frock coat and bulging waistcoat. His breeches, gaiters and collar lent him an inescapably clerical air. He removed his hat and let loose an energetic salvo of opinions.

"You understand, of course, being gentlemen who value common sense, that none of this would have happened if that damned (and I use the word advisedly Mr. Holmes), damned Liberal Government had not abolished the Church Rates. The finger of blame points firmly in the direction of Westminster," expostulated the Dean waving his hand in the general direction of the northern suburbs of the city. Holmes and I looked at each other in astonishment. I rather doubted whether Holmes was even aware of the compulsory church rates. It was probably one of those pieces of lumber that he had removed from his mental attic. The Dean, however, continued in full flight. "I am sure, Mr Holmes, that you will have been as distressed as my colleagues and myself to hear of the disappearance of the Revd. Russell. We were hoping that you would be able to help us in this matter."

Holmes held up his hand and the Dean relented for a moment "My dear sir, surely this is the domain of the moral teacher rather than the criminal investigator. You have surely misunderstood my talents. I would have thought that your colleagues and you had more of the necessary skills than an expert consulting detective like myself."

"No sir, it is you who has misunderstood, this is sadly more a question of mammon than morality. So far this fact has been concealed from the voracious editors of our yellow press, but the Revd. Russell took more than just a milkmaid and a suitcase of clothes, he also fled with one thousand pounds of church funds."

"Ah!" said Holmes. "I see. I agree that does put a different complexion on the matter. At the moment I am, however, otherwise engaged, so sadly I am unable to pursue your missing money."

The prelate was clearly taken aback. "My good sir, I am offering you a chance to be involved in investigating the case with which the whole country seems to be obsessed. Think of the fame that would offer."

"As my colleague Dr. Watson will confirm, I take cases only if they offer something of the recherché or the unusual. Even a criminal investigator of the most limited experience could offer at least ten similar cases from the last five years. I can think of at least thirty. Greedy and lustful clerics are sadly all too common."

"I have travelled all this way to see you, you will at least listen to the facts of the case and suggest anyone who may be able to help us, for example a colleague of similar standing in France."

Such a comment was bound to irritate my friend and he answered acerbically. "I will certainly listen to a brief synopsis of the case, but I will only be able to recommend one or two rather inferior agents in France. Pray proceed."

The Dean adjusted his waistcoat and puffed himself up as if about to deliver a sermon. "The Revd. Russell was, I mean is, no I mean was, a very good parish priest. He has held the living at St Martin's for almost fifteen years and never a whisper of scandal. He was always a little too Roman for my taste but these days that is scarcely a matter for suspicion anymore. He was certainly well thought of by the parishioners. I must say, however, I was surprised when he married. He must have been in his late thirties and I had always rather assumed that he had chosen celibacy after the Roman fashion. I am sure you will agree with me that some of our anglo catholics are more Roman than the Pope."

Holmes clearly had neither opinion on nor interest in the matter and motioned the Dean to continue. "The woman he married was a pretty young widow whom he met, apparently, through his cousin. The rumour went round that he had married her out of kindness, her first husband having left her little but a pile of outstanding debts. I have never believed that pity is the soundest basis for a marriage, but they appeared happy enough and she certainly took the eye of a few admirers on the occasions that I saw her."

"The first I heard of this business was from the two Churchwardens, Goulden and Hill, who marched over to the Deanery to tell me that Russell had not been seen for two days and that people were becoming a little concerned. They asked whether we would say prayers at the Cathedral. Then the next day, I learnt that the young wife had received a visit from a farmer out in Stelling Minnis, who was brandishing a note from his daughter saying that she had run off to France with the Revd. Russell and demanding to know what the church was going to do about it. At that point the Archbishop, who fortunately was in the city at the time, asked me to try and sort things out."

"I went straight over to the vicarage and found a very distressed Mrs. Russell, who told me that her husband had disappeared with a travelling bag and had not been seen for three days. She went on to confirm the story that he appeared to have run off with this farmer's daughter. Worse was to come when she informed me that Mr Bennett, the parish clerk, had called to ask her if Revd. Russell had deposited the one thousand pounds he had drawn from their existing bank account into the new parish account. To which, it goes without saying, the answer was no."

Holmes maintained his stony but attentive silence, however, I could not resist asking how the Revd. Russell had managed to secure such a sum.

"Very simply, it seems he told the gullible Mr. Bennett some cock and bull story about the manager of their existing bank, the Southern Counties, being a drunkard and a gambler and that it was improper to continue to hold the parish accounts with him. Complete nonsense, of course, Harvey is an irascible old fellow, but he is as straight as you or me. Heaven knows why Bennett should just go along with the story, but there it is." He threw his arms heavenwards in a gesture of exasperation at the stupidity of his fellow human beings.

"So, is that the complete account?" asked Holmes.

"Pretty much, after that I travelled out to Stelling Minnis to confirm the farmer's story, but it seems true enough. I saw a note in her childish and misspelt hand saying that she had run away to France with the Revd. Russell and offering some feeble excuses about love. Typical girlish piffle if you ask me."

"I returned to find that the papers had heard of the story and were gathering fine copy at our expense. The police have been very little help, they say that once they reach France the felons are out of their jurisdiction. In my opinion they are enjoying our discomfiture as much as anyone else. I implore you Mr. Holmes, will you not even glance at the case?"

Holmes stood up slowly and moved across to his desk. He pulled down a reference volume, wrote two names on a slip of paper and handed it to the Dean. "These are agents that I have had contact with in France. They are both good and trustworthy men but of limited ability. They are the best France has to offer, I fear."

"I am grateful, but do you have no advice to give me?" the Dean asked again.

Holmes sat back in his chair by the fireplace and lapsed into his characteristic pensive position, fingers templed before his lips. After some five minutes, he sat up and I sensed that he was on the point of saying something of significance to the Dean, but instead he shook his head and said "No, there is insufficient data, it would, as Watson will tell you, be a capital error to offer you what could easily be misleading musings."

ADVERTISEMENTS.

WHAT IS CANTERBURY FAMOUS FOR?

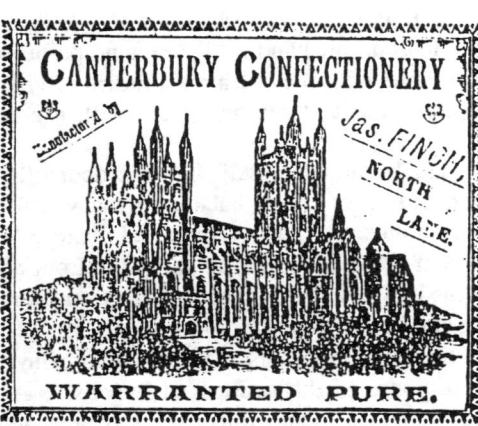

High-Class   **Kentish Jams**

MARMALADE A SPECIALITY.

Visitors should ask their Grocers for

Finch, Son, & Co.'s
MANUFACTURES,

Which are Noted for their Purity; and should not forget to carry a supply home with them.

The Dean demurred, clearly disappointed. He rose, picked up his hat, bowed to us both, and left, pausing only to say "You have my card, if you do have any further suggestions please contact me."

Holmes nodded and as the door shut, he slumped back into his favourite chair beside the fireplace and resumed his introspective mood. He sat like that for over an hour. Finally, he perceptibly shook himself, rose from the chair and said "No Watson, it is no good, there are simply not enough facts. And yet, and yet and yet... there is something about this story that nags away at me."

"I have to say that it all seems very clear to me..."

"Stop." Holmes held up his hand. "There is no point in discussing it. Put your coat on and come with me. I have a desire to visit my haunts in Limehouse and drive the scent of religiosity out with a good blast of salt air."

But no sooner had I readied myself than the doorbell sounded again and we were to find ourselves thrust back into the world of clerics and cathedrals by the appearance of a most unexpected visitor. Downstairs we could hear the sounds of the housekeeper opening the front door and female voices muttering in the hall. Soft footsteps slowly ascended the stairs.

"A young woman of good class I would say, Watson," Holmes said. I smiled, but had no time to pursue his methods, before my colleague was calling "Enter!" in response to the gentlest of knocks. A charming but extremely distressed woman of about thirty years of age, tentatively came into the room. She was, like the Dean, dressed in black from head to toe, but she wore her dress and veil with far greater elegance. Holmes took her gently by the hand and led her to the chair opposite him by the fireplace.

"Please sit down Mrs. Russell," he said. "I am sure you must be very distressed by the disappearance of your husband."

The young woman gasped. "How did you know who I was Mr. Holmes? You are Mr Holmes are you not?"

"I am, and this is my valued colleague Dr. Watson. As to how I identified you, it is a relatively simple matter if you have the return portion of a train ticket to Canterbury tucked into your glove and are clasping a letter in the hand of the Dean of the Cathedral addressed to Mrs. Russell." The young woman looked relieved that at least this apparently miraculous display of powers had a human explanation. "Now Mrs. Russell," said Holmes. "How can I help you?"

"I doubt you can help me. I doubt if anyone can help me. Other than the good Lord," she corrected herself. "I assume you have read the details of this ... this ghastly business." We both nodded.

"My husband was a..." she paused for a moment as if searching for exactly the right word. "...a very kindly man. I will not conceal the fact that we did not marry for love. It was an act of necessity on my part following the death of my first husband who turned out to be heavily in debt. I met Mr. Russell through his cousin, Angela, who had offered me a room in her house in Wiltshire. When he learnt of my plight he immediately offered marriage. I was much surprised by the offer but after a day's thought and some conversation with dear Angela, I assented and we were wed within days."

I have often said that Holmes could be the most gallant of gentlemen to women in distress. He spoke to Mrs. Russell in the kindest of manners, but still asked what others would have considered impertinences. "Was your union a happy one?"

"Until just recently, I had believed that it was, Mr. Holmes. He was very different from my first husband who had been an inveterate sportsman and gambler. Mr. Russell was very gentle and considerate. He seemed genuinely grateful for my company. In the long winter evenings we would sit by the fire in his small study and read from the scriptures or books of sermons. I would not have believed him to be the kind of man who would run off with a milkmaid. I was so shocked and surprised when I learnt that..." she stumbled again searching for the right word as the emotion of her tale seemed to grip her "...that this thing was happening. I could not believe it. But who can understand the ways of the heart?"

"How did you first learn of this liaison?" asked Holmes.

"Mr Bennett, the parish clerk, intimated his suspicions in a private interview that he had sought from me about three weeks ago."

"Ah, the parish clerk!" said Holmes in an attempt to break the heavy atmosphere in the room. "In my experience Watson the parish clerk is usually second to no-one in matters of self-importance. Is that so in this case Mrs. Russell?"

"Well, it is difficult to say. Mr. Bennett is a very particular man, extremely careful over matters touching the parish accounts. He is also very abstemious and devout which can give him an air of stiffness, but he has been very careful to attend to my needs in this difficult time. I know that he will have been very upset about the theft of this money and may even consider it to be his fault."

"And how had the good Mr. Bennett learnt of the existence of this young woman?"

"As I understand it, the clerk also looks after the accounts of a number of farmers in the countryside surrounding the city. He told me that on a trip to Stelling Minnis he had seen my husband together with this young woman. He did not give me any details of what he had observed, and indeed, I am not sure I would have wished to hear them. He simply suggested that their relationship seemed to be closer than that which would be expected between a clergyman in my husband's position and a young woman."

"Did you confront your husband with these suspicions?" asked Holmes.

"No, he has been so generous to me and I suppose I just could not believe that it was true," she replied.

"Had your husband given you any cause for suspicion?" I interjected. "Were you aware for example, that he had been going out to this village, whatever it was called?"

"No. He gave me no cause for any concern. He seemed completely unchanged. As to visiting Stelling Minnis, it is some seven or eight miles off, but he has a pony and trap and is often out visiting parishioners all day so it is possible, but as I say he was a kindly man."

"Were you aware that the money was also missing?" asked Holmes.

For a fleeting instant I sensed a slight stiffening in her manner and perhaps a slight reddening of the cheeks but she answered very directly "Yes, I knew about the concerns over Mr. Harvey and was aware that my husband and Mr. Bennett were going to close the accounts, but I could never have imagined that he would make off with the money."

"The parish clerk, Mr. Bennett, how long has he held that post?" asked Holmes.

"I believe about four years. He came south from somewhere in the Midlands where he had had a number of successful business interests. He settled here and became a stalwart member of the church. I understand that my husband felt his business knowledge made him an excellent candidate for parish clerk."

"Thank you for your very clear account of the matter Mrs. Russell. I am very touched by your obvious distress but I am not clear how I may be of service to you?" said Holmes.

"I am not sure that I know myself. I learnt that the Dean was coming to see you and immediately felt that you were the last best hope of finding my husband and wanted to come and urge you myself to take up the case." She stood up and readied herself to leave. "If I can be of any assistance, I am at your disposal gentlemen."

The Missing Cleric

As Holmes walked her to the door I was astounded to hear him say "I will certainly look into the disappearance of your husband and may need to call on you at some future date, however, I cannot promise you a happy solution to this matter." She nodded her assent, made a gesture of farewell to each of us and then was gone.

For a moment we listened in silence to her walking down the stairs. Then as the front door closed, Holmes laughed, rubbed his hands together with glee and said to me "Now Watson, are you ready for a trip to the ancient city of Canterbury?"

"Of course, but I thought you felt this was a simple morality tale. You see something more in it now?"

"I see nothing clearly, but I fear that this tale may prove to be very much darker than the comic opera we have seen so far. There are at least six facts which make me question the validity of the accepted story, but lest I overplay my hand I will give you only one, albeit one which will appeal to your sensibilities Watson."

"I can see absolutely nothing contradictory," I replied.

"I am sure you are mistaken. Come now, what did you think to yourself when that young woman walked into the room?"

"I really do not recall, Holmes." I replied.

"Oh Watson, you disappoint me. Did you not think 'what a fine attractive-looking woman'?" I smiled vaguely and indicated assent with a reluctant wave of my hands. Holmes continued "Did you not also think what a foolish cleric it would be to flee to France with a milkmaid when he could stay in Canterbury with such a wife? The truth now Watson!"

"As ever Holmes you have divined my very thoughts," I replied with a tone of slight annoyance.

"It was not a difficult task. The exact same thoughts ran through my head. You, of course, saw them as the everyday thoughts of a man of the world. I, however, saw them as the first links in a chain of scientific reasoning. You held the data in your hand but failed to recognise them."

"That is all very well, Holmes, but that hardly turns this into a case that demands the attentions of a consulting detective."

"No, not that fact alone, but as I said there are at least five others which, put together, nag away at me. I will not bore you with them at the moment. Instead, we must lose no time in heading to Canterbury. Pack your bags and if you would be so good will you bring the volume of my index for the letter P.

We reached Charing Cross just in time to board the South Eastern Railway Company's evening train to Canterbury West with a pile of papers under our arms. Our reading added nothing to our knowledge of the case other than that the fleeing couple had been sighted in Luxembourg and that the papers generally seemed to be losing interest in the chase. Holmes settled back into the corner of our first class compartment and for the rest of the journey he expounded on the development of church music since the reformation. His exposition was, as ever, as knowledgeable as it was witty.

We arrived at Canterbury on one of those brilliant summer evenings which conspire to make this the most blessed nation on earth. In the distance church bells could be heard peeling as the ringers practised their Sunday chimes. As we walked out through the fluted pillars of the station's entrance, a battered old cocking cart with its drivers perched precariously above the horses, swayed along its slow way with its cargo of a pack of gun dogs in preparation for some rural entertainment. I pointed it out to Holmes. "You do not see sights like that in London."

"Yes, but rural charm does not prevent our country cousins committing the most cruel and violent of crimes."

"I assume that this case does not figure under that heading," I replied. Yet instead of the expected assent, all I received in reply was a curt "Data Watson data!"

We strolled down through the ancient Westgate and along the main street past its gabled huguenot cottages, tudor buildings and medieval hospital. Holmes said little on our stroll and I was content to drink in the atmosphere, but I sensed an anxiety in his demeanour which I had not expected.

We took rooms at the Flying Horse Inn on Dover Street. Holmes seeming to feel satisfied that this particular hostelry was strategically placed for his inquiries. For my part, I was content that it offered clean sheets and served a fine pint of Flint and Sons' local ales. We ate a good meal, but Holmes remained terse throughout. As we separated to go to our rooms all he would say was "At present, I would prefer our presence here to be unknown to the principle players in the drama." He then left me to attend to his index book and a small pile of telegram forms that he had secured on our journey.

The next morning, we both rose early and ate an excellent breakfast of bacon and eggs. Then after a silent pipe each, I asked Holmes what he intended to do. "My dear Watson, yours is the key part today. I intend to don the guise of a tourist and visit a few of the delightful churches in the city. You, on the other hand, will travel out to Stelling Minnis and discover what you can about the alluring milkmaid." Holmes pushed a map across the table and traced the route along Stone Street, the old Roman Road, towards Hythe and the southern ports. I nodded that I understood the way and folded the map into my pocket. Holmes continued his instructions. "I want you to pay particular attention to two points. First, how many people had seen the young woman with Revd. Russell and second, but most important, I want you to secure a word for word transcript of the note she left. This is of signal importance."

"That is all perfectly clear," I said.

"Any other information you secure will be a bonus but fail on those two points and the trip will have been so much wasted effort." Holmes spoke with insistent authority and I knew that he would accept nothing less than complete compliance with his requirements. With that he stood up, wished me well and turned on his heel to attend to his own affairs. I set out on my journey.

That evening I returned a more fatigued, more dishevelled and much muddier fellow than I had been that morning. I found Holmes sitting in a corner of the bar enjoying a leisurely pipe. He greeted me cheerily, waved me into an armchair and offered me his tobacco. Nonetheless he was clearly concerned mainly to hear news of my inquiries. "Well Watson, you look as if you have truly sampled the country air. I am sure that it will have improved your health and well-being, but what have you learnt about our milkmaid?"

"I have learnt many things, but principally that country folk can tell a city-dweller at a hundred paces and believe that his pockets are invariably lined with gold or at least a copious quantity of silver."

"I fear Watson that you may have shown too much interest. Have I not always told you that the surest way of securing a piece of information is to show no interest in it whatsoever?"

"I did try to bear that in mind, but there have been so many people asking about the couple that all visitors are suspected of being interested in that one affair."

"So did you learn anything of importance?" asked Holmes with a certain exasperation.

"I believe so. The young woman, Sarah Black, was certainly rumoured to have been having a liaison with someone she described as a 'very learned man'. Everyone was willing to tell me that for free. I had to dispense a veritable pocketful of silver to learn any more.

"I started off, as I hope you would have done, by directing myself to the landlord of the nearest inn, the "Old Dog". He was a surly fellow until I slipped a sovereign across the bar to pay for my pint of stout. His tongue then became as loose as one of his customers who has had one too many of these local ales. He told me that Miss Black was a bad sort. I doubt if she was the sort of woman that Revd. Russell would have met in his church. She was found more often outside the inn having enjoyed some of its wares."

"Had the landlord heard her speak of the fellow?"

"He had certainly heard her boasting that she was engaged to a man of distinction and would soon marry. Although he had never heard her speak his name directly, he was pleased to boast that he had known the identity of her suitor even before she fled. Apparently she had confided the name to the landlord's daughter, who had promptly made it public."

"By this time," I continued. "A group of half a dozen farmhands and tradesmen had gathered round the bar and by the judicious purchase of a few jars of ale they were happily drawn into the conversation, but they added little other than confirmation of the landlord's tale. I pressed my informants as to whether anyone had actually seen the reverend gentleman together with Miss Black. One or two suggested that they thought they might have seen them together, but none were very convincing. So after a further purchase of refreshments, I took my leave and followed the directions I had been given to Miss Black's family home."

"I found the house, after much effort, down the end of a very narrow and muddy lane. The Black's work for one of the local farmers. They are clearly a poor and ill-educated family, but the cottage although small and cramped was tidy and clean. Inside I found a distraught mother and an outraged father. They were very unfriendly at first, but when they learned that I was intent on finding their daughter they became more helpful. They seemed genuinely concerned about their daughter's well-being."

"They told me that their daughter had been telling them that she was going to improve their lot in the near future, a promise that they treated with unsurprising scepticism. They claim, and I believe them, that they had no inkling of what was going on between their daughter and the clergyman. So it came as a complete shock to them when they came back from a trip to Canterbury market one day and found a note saying that their daughter had run off to France with the Revd. Russell."

"And did you see the note? It is essential that I know what the note said," urged Holmes.

"I had to buy some rather expensive eggs and bread, but the appearance of a few coins encouraged the father to show me the note which I then copied down as you asked." I pushed the paper across to Holmes with a certain pride at having completed his tasks to the letter.

He picked it up and read it aloud *"Dear Ma and Pa The Revd. Russell of St Martin's Canterbury and I are in love. We have decided to fly together to France. I know our union is forbidden but I believe true love absolves everything. I will arrange for funds to be sent to you from France. Your loving daughter Sarah."*

Holmes paused for a second as if absorbing the note's full contents. "Excellent, this seems to confirm my suspicions. Could Miss Black read and write?" he asked.

"Her parents were barely literate and had to ask a neighbour to read the note, but I can not say for certain whether Miss Black was also illiterate."

"You should certainly have pursued that most vital piece of information, Watson. Was the note neatly written?"

"No it was most abominably written. At points it was very hard to decipher the letters. I should have said that Miss Black was a decidedly ill-educated young woman."

"Did she take any clothes with her for the trip?" he asked abruptly changing the subject.

"Again I do not know, Holmes. After copying down the note, I felt that there was little else I could learn from the Blacks, so I took my leave as quickly as possible," I replied.

"Well, you seem to have done reasonably well, but you should have paid more attention to those last two points Watson," said Holmes.

I bridled at that grudging praise and responded with asperity. "Well, what have you done with your day?"

"I seem to have upset you. That was not my intention. I am sure that my endeavours will seem less relevant and less arduous than your own, but I assure you that I have ascertained certain facts which put together with your information has greatly clarified the situation."

"So, what have you done?"

"I spent the morning sitting here reading my index book. I then read two telegrams that I received from Lincoln. In the afternoon, I visited a church and explored some of the burial practices of our ancestors and this evening I went to a small bookshop in Mercery Lane and bought you this small volume. I think it will help you to better understand our little problem." Holmes handed me a copy of a volume from the early part of the century entitled *Crabbe's Works*. I stared at the leather bound book for a moment with some annoyance and then asked "So what is our next move?"

"Tonight Watson, you shall have a bath and then we shall stroll into town and take a meal at the Cathedral Restaurant where I understand they serve the most excellent fish from the nearby coastal fisheries. Tomorrow we have an appointment with Mr Bennett, the esteemed parish clerk, in order to ascertain how he managed to allow one thousand pounds to slip through his fingers."

The next morning dawned fine and bright and it was a pleasure to be up and about after the previous day's exertions. We walked across the city, observing its own particular sights such as a group of cathedral choristers in their caps, wide collars and jackets, their surplices over their arms hustling past us en route to practise in the cathedral.

Mr. Bennett lived in a red-brick three storey house on the north-eastern side of the town just outside the Cathedral precincts. We rang the bell and the door was opened swiftly by a tall man of about forty-five years. "Mr. Holmes, I assume, and of course this is Dr. Watson. Your reputation goes before you. Come in." His manner was affable but I sensed a certain anxiety. Holmes, I noticed had grasped him firmly by the hand and was shaking it in a surprisingly effusive manner. We were shown into a sparsely furnished study, whose walls were lined with books and ledgers. We sat cramped together on a small settee while Mr Bennett sat himself behind his desk.

"I am sorry to trouble you at such trying time, but I just need to clarify the details of the manner by which the reverend gentleman managed to secure one thousand pounds of church funds for his own use."

Bennett shuffled the papers on his desk, while he considered how to start his account. "To begin with Mr. Holmes, I must tell you that the exact sum in question was one thousand and fifty six pounds seven shillings and fourpence." Holmes waved his hand as if to dismiss this trifling detail, but the treasurer was insistent. "I appreciate such points must seem trivial to you, but they are the very lifeblood of the financial mind."

Holmes demurred and Bennett continued. "The money, as you may have heard, was almost the total funds in the parish accounts. It comprised monies belonging to the Ladies' Bible Class, the Choral Class, the Coffee Tavern, the Temperance Society, various charitable funds, and above all funds to be used to undertake essential repairs to the fabric and structure of the church. You will understand, of course, that the building itself is very old, have you seen the plans for the proposed renovations?" He suddenly digressed gesturing at a pile of papers.

To my surprise Holmes leapt up and proceeded to pore over the drawings with our meticulous and particular host. My friend kept stretching to point to different features and enquire as to the exact dimensions of a window or door. Finally he seemed to exhaust the possible points of interest in the plan and sat down again. I sensed, however, that Holmes had been frustrated in some ulterior motive.

ADVERTISEMENTS.

PERFUMER TO H.R.H. THE PRINCESS OF WALES AND H.R.H. PRINCESS CHRISTIAN.

BY APPOINTMENT.

JOHN R. HALL'S
WOOD VIOLET.

"Has a very decided and durable violet scent."—*The Queen.*

PATRONISED BY

H.R.H. THE PRINCESS OF WALES.
H.R.H. PRINCESS CHRISTIAN.

H.R.H. the PRINCESS LOUISE (Marchioness of Lorne).
H.R.H. PRINCESS HENRY OF BATTENBERG.
H.R.H. the HEREDITARY PRINCESS OF SAXE-MEININGEN.
H.R.H. PRINCESS FREDERICK LEOPOLD OF PRUSSIA.
H.I.H. the GRAND DUCHESS OF MECKLENBERG-SCHWERIN.
H.R.H. the COUNTESS OF FLANDERS.
H.G.D.H. PRINCESS LOUIS OF BATTENBERG.
H.S.H. the PRINCESS CAROLINA MATILDA OF SCHLESWIG-HOLSTEIN.
H.S.H. PRINCESS EDWARD OF SAXE-WEIMAR.
H.S.H. the DUCHESS OF SCHLESWIG-HOLSTEIN.
H.S.H. the PRINCESS HENRY OF PLESS.

In Bottles, 1/6, 2/6, 4/6, 8/6, 10/6, and 21/-. Globe Shape, 1/6, 2/6, 5/6, 7/6, 10/6, and 21/-. Sachets, 1/-, 2/-, and 3/6.

PROPRIETOR—
EDWIN R. BIGGLESTON, MERCERY LANE, CANTERBURY.

Mr. Bennett turned the conversation back to the disappearance of the funds. "Late last month the Revd. Russell came to me and told me that he was concerned that Mr Harvey, the manager at our bank was a man whose personal habits were not suitable for the custodian of church funds and suggested that we transfer the money from the Southern Counties. I must say I was reluctant to do this, such transfers always cause problems with payments for a while afterwards."

"Yet you agreed?" asked Holmes.

"I could do little else. I must say I shared some of the Revd. Russell's concerns about Mr. Harvey, and in the end it has to be his decision, so I accepted. He volunteered to make the actual transfer of funds and again I failed to resist this offer. You will understand that I little expected him to take out the sum in cash and then to disappear with the money." Our host threw his arms in the air in a gesture of resignation.

Holmes coughed just as he was about to reply and something seemed to catch in his throat. All at once he was coughing and choking violently. He doubled over quite red in the face and indicated desperately that he needed water. Mr. Bennett immediately rushed out to find a glass. In an instant Holmes stood up, dashed across the room and tore a handful of pieces of paper from the pile on the desk and thrust them in his pocket. He turned and winked at me and then resumed his incapacitated pose.

With the help of a little water Holmes was soon sitting up again and telling the perplexed Bennett that he was prone to these attacks and that all was now well. "Thank you" he said placing the glass on the desk. "We will not take much more of your precious time but I wonder if you would allow me to take a glance at the accounts for the restoration fund before we leave?"

Mr. Bennett looked as surprised as I was at the request. I had seen the ledger prominently on the top shelf by the desk but could not imagine what Holmes would learn from it. Mr. Bennett seemed happy to comply and reached up and pulled down the relevant volume. My colleague leafed through the pages and stared intently at a few entries and then snapped it shut. "Thank you," he said. "We must be going now, you have been most helpful."

"Is that all?" asked the clerk somewhat confused by my friend's methods. "Do you hold out any hope of finding the absent Revd. Russell and, of course, the money?"

"I cannot say," replied Holmes. "This is a most unusual case. Good morning Mr. Bennett." With that he picked up his hat and left with me following in his wake.

The Missing Cleric

Once outside I made to question Holmes on what he had learnt from the parish clerk, but all he would say was "Let us go up to St Martin's Church itself, but I beg a few minutes of silence as we walk. I need to plan our next steps with great care."

St. Martin's sat, perhaps appropriately as it turned out, just beyond the county jail on the slope of the hill along the road to the ancient port of Sandwich. Above it stood a fine, although sadly no longer functioning, windmill. The church itself is one of the most ancient in the city. It has its roots back in Saxon times and legend has it that St. Augustine preached there. Its churchyard is filled with white crosses, ancient gravestones and some more recent bedstead grave markers. Holmes motioned me to sit down next to him on one of the ancient tombs and for a while we simply sat there, Holmes lost in his thoughts, and I, for my part, admiring the wonderful view down to the Cathedral. At last he shook himself from his reverie. "Now Watson do you see the point to which this investigation is inexorably leading. I assume you grasp the problem of actually proving the matter." Holmes spoke in a matter of fact manner.

"I understand almost nothing about this business. I would have thought that if we wanted to recover the funds and find the missing clergyman we would need to be in France. Yet, I sense that you perceive things about this affair that are completely hidden to me."

Holmes groaned and wiped his forehead. "Well, I see I will have to lay the facts before you with more care." I nodded but Holmes went on, "First, however, we must undertake a small test which will determine the future course of this case. Do you have a pencil old fellow?"

I produced a thick black pencil from my pocket and Holmes set to stripping away the wooden stem with his pocket knife, leaving only the graphite centre. He then placed it on a sheet of paper and proceeded to crush the graphite to a powder with a handy stone. Finally he produced from his pocket the sheets he had removed from Mr. Bennett's desk. "These are telegram forms," said Holmes. "My belief is that the parish clerk will have had to wire to France in the last few days. My hope is that any message will have left some vague imprint on the forms immediately underneath."

He took the top sheet and placed it on the gravestone that was serving as a table. He gently sprinkled the graphite over the white form and rocked it across the surface of the paper. "Now, let us see what this reveals," he said and carefully blew the excess graphite onto the ground. "Eureka!" he said with real triumph and satisfaction in his voice. "What do you think to that Watson?" On the previously blank form, I could just see the shapes of letters picked out in black dust.

"The message is virtually illegible but that is unimportant," said Holmes. "The address can be very readily reconstructed." He took out his notebook and transcribed what he saw. "Mlle. L. Austin, L'Hôtel Hirondelle, Rue St Jérôme, Paris. We have him Watson. The man is ours. I must go to the telegraph office at once."

"But Holmes, you have still to explain what all this is about," I said in exasperation.

"I am sorry Watson, but I feel we have to act at once. You must take the next train to London and return as soon as possible with our pistols and, if possible, Lestrade from the Yard. Tell him what you like but persuade him to come. I will go and send these telegrams and alert the local constabulary. You must meet me back here no later than eight o'clock this evening. Is that clear?" asked Holmes.

"I will do as you say," I replied.

"One more thing, I would be grateful if you would approach the church by a circuitous route to ensure that you are seen by as few people as possible." With that instruction we parted.

My journey to London and back was a trying one. Cattle had strayed on to the line near Maidstone and the train was delayed for almost half an hour as they were cleared away by a slow-moving farmhand. Once in London, I went straight to Scotland Yard, only to find that Lestrade was absent and that no-one could inform me as to his whereabouts or when he was likely to return. I left the Inspector a note informing him of the imminent denouement of Holmes' latest investigation and suggested that he meet me at Charing Cross at 5pm, but I feared that I might return to Canterbury alone that evening.

Worse was to follow. I arrived in Baker Street at exactly the same moment as a potential client. He was a young man with the absurd name of Augustus Buckskin-Popham and he wanted help with a complex case of fraud. In spite of my protestations and promises that Holmes would attend to the matter on his return, he continued to insist on laying the outline of the matter before me and then to clarify abstruse details which he expected me to pass on to Holmes. As a result I only just reached the station on time. To my great joy, I found Lestrade waiting at the gate.

As we rattled our way though south east London I explained what I could of the matter, but ultimately we both resigned ourselves to awaiting Holmes' revelations. "All I can say Doctor," sighed Lestrade, "is that there is no-one else who could persuade me to run down to the Kent countryside at the drop of a hat, but Holmes always makes it worth my while."

We arrived in good time and took a long circuitous route, partly across fields and orchards, to the church. At first we assumed that Holmes had yet to arrive, everything seemed so still and peaceful. As we walked across the apparently deserted graveyard a voice hissed at us with urgency, "Lestrade! Watson! Over here quickly!" We followed the familiar voice behind a group of small bushes standing against the wall of the cemetery. Behind the bush was Holmes and next to him was a burly man, who despite, his tweed suit, was clearly a policeman. "Welcome, " said Holmes. "This is Inspector Roberts of the Kent Constabulary."

"It's good to meet you two gentlemen," the policeman said with a heavy country burr to his voice. "But I can't rightly say what I make of all this. I can't help thinking that this will turn out to be a wild goose chase."

To Holmes' obvious pleasure Lestrade immediately replied in the most positive of tones. "I can assure you Inspector that if Mr Holmes is leading the chase, it will not be after wild geese. But I would be grateful, Holmes, if you could enlighten us as to what in heaven's name we are waiting for?"

"Your question is just," replied Holmes in a hushed voice. "I have kept you, and especially Watson, in the dark for far too long. You will have realised that we are not investigating a simple case of adultery, nor even a straightforward theft. This, I am afraid, is murder."

I can still recall the chill that those words brought to Lestrade and me. The evening suddenly felt colder and darker and we both held our silence for a long moment before bursting out, almost together, with the obvious questions. "But who has been murdered? Where is the body and who is the murderer?"

"Think for a moment Watson, and the answer to the first question will become obvious."

As Holmes suggested I considered the facts and then said very carefully "Well as only Revd. Russell and Miss Black are missing it must be one of them." Holmes nodded encouragingly. "And if we assume that the woman in the Paris hotel is Miss Black, then presumably the absent clergyman is dead."

"Excellent Watson."

"Oh how cruel!" I exclaimed. "Doubly cruel! Not only to be murdered but then to have your reputation destroyed as well. That is murder indeed."

"And the murderer?" asked Lestrade.

"Apparently Mr. Holmes believes it to be Mr Bennett, the parish clerk," said Roberts. "I only hope that you can prove this. I must say it seems very unlikely to me. After all you can't even tell us where the body lies."

"My hope," explained Holmes, "is that we can lure him here and confront the man with his crimes. I have had a telegram sent to him from the hotel in Paris where Miss Black is staying, using her assumed name. The message says that she is now aware of his true identity and that he must meet her father here at the church this evening to come to some arrangement or he will be exposed to the police. We have been fortunate in persuading one of Roberts' constables to play the role of Miss Black's father." Holmes indicated a previously unnoticed figure standing in the shadows of the church porch.

"Astounding," I said.

"I must add," said Holmes, "that I believe Miss Black to be a wholly innocent party to this matter. She is sadly under the illusion that she will be starting a new relationship with the former Revd. Russell of St Martin's, Canterbury. I am certain that Bennett wooed her under that guise and has made all sorts of persuasive promises to her. My other sadness is that Mrs. Russell may also have had a part, albeit unwittingly, in the events that led up to this tragedy."

"At what time do you expect Bennett to arrive?" asked the practical Lestrade.

Holmes consulted his watch and was on the point of speaking when we noticed a dark figure coming at some speed across the graveyard. "Inspector!" called a country voice. "Inspector where are you?"

"It's one of my men," said Roberts. "Something must have happened." We all tumbled out of our cramped hiding place to see what was afoot. A small red faced constable was standing there, breathing heavily.

"He's gone," he panted. "Bennett's just gone and taken a pony and trap and set off down the Dover Road."

"Damn!" said Holmes. "I knew we were dealing with a clever man. It is just as well we planned for such a contingency. Where is that carriage I asked you to have standing by, Roberts?"

"It's just up there," he replied and pointed to a spot a short way up the hill. Roberts took his constable's whistle and blew a few short blasts in a pre-arranged signal.

"Do you think we can catch him?" asked Lestrade.

"How long ago did he leave?" Roberts asked his constable.

"No more than a quarter hour, sir. I came as soon as he left," he replied.

"I believe we have a good chance, although we will be heavier than his carriage we have better horses," said Roberts who seemed to relish the idea of a chase.

"More to the point," added Holmes, "he is unaware that he is being pursued, so he may not be flying at top speed." The carriage drew up by the church gate and we four climbed in.

"The driver will try and take us on a route that will bring us down on to the Dover Road without going back on ourselves, then we will chase him like he had the very devil on his tail," said Roberts with glee.

Holmes was in a state of high anxiety as we set off. We bounced and swayed precariously along a cross country route in a manner which left Holmes cursing both the lack of speed and the danger of too hasty progress. On one occasion we had to stop to open a gate and I could hear Holmes cursing to himself under his breath. We crossed rutted tracks and heard branches scratching at the side of the carriage, but after what seemed like an eternity we joined the Dover Road and the chase began in earnest.

Twenty minutes later Roberts spied a carriage light up ahead and our expectations were wildly aroused as we approached it. It turned out to be only a farmer on his way home, but he confirmed that there was a trap just a short way ahead. The driver pushed on, and I could hear the panting of the horses in between the creak of the harness and the clip of the hooves. Outside night had long since fallen but a sliver of moon allowed the shadowy forms of trees and bushes to be discerned on either side. The light of an occasional cottage home would slip by, the warmth of the image contrasting strongly with the cold of the service revolver in my coat pocket.

"I see him," shouted Roberts at last. "He's not carrying any lights so we are almost on top of him." We all craned out of the windows and there was a pony and trap answering the exact description we had been given. As we drew alongside we could see Bennett's face in the light of our lamp and I caught the look of surprise as we hailed him to stop.

The trap pulled up without resistance and the local Inspector turned to us and said "Now gentlemen, this is a police matter and I would ask you all to stay here. I will see if I can persuade him to come back to the city with us on a voluntary basis. If not, I may need to call on your aid. I must say Mr. Holmes, that in the absence of your little ruse back at the church, I do not see what evidence we have with which I can compel him to return."

"Fear not, Inspector, if you and I cannot persuade him to return, Lestrade will certainly do the trick," said Holmes with an air of mystery. "All I would say, is that no matter what the appearances may be, you must keep your firearms close at hand."

We could hear the vague murmur of voices as Roberts confronted the clerk. The conversation sounded very calm and reasonable. After a few minutes, Roberts returned with a defeated expression on his face. "I am afraid he is very insistent that he is on important and urgent business and would prefer not to come back to the city tonight. He readily admits receiving your telegram, but says he made neither head nor tail of it. He even admits to carrying a large sum of money in cash, but says that it is connected with his business. I have to say, Mr. Holmes, that I do not believe that my superiors would take it kindly if I compelled a respected member of the public to come back with us without solid evidence."

"I understand your problem Inspector, but may I try and resolve it for you?" said Holmes. "Lestrade, you stay in the shadow of the carriage but take a good look at this man." As we alighted Holmes whispered to me to move to the far side of the trap and keep my hand on my revolver. My colleague strolled over and greeted Mr. Bennett with a cheery "Good evening."

"Good evening Mr. Holmes," replied Bennett stiffly but with no apparent air of concern. "I understand you wish to talk to me again about the flight of Revd. Russell and the theft of the money. I am, as I hope the Inspector told you, in something of a hurry. I wonder if we might discuss this tomorrow?"

"I do not wish to discuss the man's flight. I wish to discuss his murder," said Holmes bluntly.

"Murder?" Bennett seemed genuinely surprised. "Are you suggesting I had some hand in this?"

"That is what I wish to discuss," replied Holmes giving particular emphasis to the "I".

"You are making a dreadful mistake. What evidence do you have that I killed the Revd. Russell?"

"I have no substantial evidence that you murdered him," said Holmes calmly. As he spoke I felt suddenly crestfallen at the prospect of seeing our man escape, but my colleague continued with complete command. "My only hope is that before you go to the gallows, which you assuredly will, you will have the decency to tell us where you have hidden the body of the Revd. Bennett so that he may receive a deserved Christian burial."

"Mr. Holmes you are making no sense. You have no evidence that I murdered Russell. You admit that you have no corpse. So by what right are you going to compel me to come back to Canterbury with you?" asked Bennett.

"I cannot compel you," said Holmes.

"But I can," said another voice. Lestrade stepped out of the shadow and walked straight up to Bennett. As he did, I saw Holmes pull out his revolver and I followed his example.

"John Paxton," the London policeman said, "I charge you with the murder of a prison guard while escaping from Lincoln prison seven years ago and it is my duty to take you back to that prison where I have no doubt that the sentence of death already passed on you for previous crimes will be carried out."

The erstwhile clerk suddenly sprang forward as if to attempt escape. Holmes instantly shouted "Have no compunction about shooting Watson. He is a most dangerous creature."

With that the villain seemed to become aware of the revolvers trained on him and he slumped back into his seat in a crumpled heap. I have rarely seen a man so thoroughly defeated. Roberts, to his credit, was instant in his response and swiftly had the murderer in handcuffs and was soon leading him to the carriage. Lestrade stood half shocked, half triumphant staring after the now bent figure.

"Well that is certainly a triumph for Sherlock Holmes. To capture Paxton, the man who cheated and murdered two Lincolnshire clergymen in the early eighties, is indeed a success."

Holmes smiled. "I am quite content with the achievement itself. I would think that as far as the press are concerned Roberts and yourself can share the credit. All I ask is that you two gentlemen join Watson and me in the bar of the Flying Horse tomorrow lunchtime, so that we may discuss the finer points of the case."

The two policemen gladly assented and then travelled off in the carriage. Holmes and I took Bennett's trap and travelled quietly and at a leisurely pace back to Canterbury. As we passed through the old city walls Holmes said "You should have read that little book I purchased for you. You would have learnt that there is nothing new under the sun. Crabbe tells the tale of a parish clerk who resisted all the assaults of the devil but could not shrink from the temptation of putting his hand into the church coffers and helping himself." I laughed and then we both fell silent again contemplating the deeds of the last few days.

At one o'clock the next day we were all together again in the bar of the Flying Horse. Roberts and Lestrade immediately reported the sad news that the Revd. Russell had indeed been murdered and more ghoulishly that his body had been hidden in one of the family graves at his own church. They were also able to report on the safe imprisonment of Paxton, as we now called him, which led Holmes to begin to explain the train of logic that had brought him to such astounding conclusions.

"As Watson will gladly tell you, I took little interest in this matter at first. It seemed nothing more than scandal and tittle-tattle. It was only when the Dean forced the affair on my attention and revealed the financial aspect to the case that I began to take notice. I immediately thought of the Paxton case. I knew that he was at large and that one day we would come across his traces, but at that point there was very little data."

"However, the visit of Mrs. Russell renewed my concern that there might be more to this case than adultery. As I said to Watson, I felt it unlikely that a man of such religious convictions, recently married to such a charming woman, would fly off with a milkmaid. I was intrigued by the appearance in the story of the parish clerk who had both access to the money and had suggested to Mrs Russell that her husband was being unfaithful. He seemed immediately to be a central factor in the case."

"I also sensed that Mrs. Russell was concerned about some aspect of the case that she did not specify. Why did she come hurrying up to London as soon as she learnt that the Dean would visit me? She had seemed somewhat uneasy over the matter of the money and I did wonder if she and the clerk were in league. I went to visit the unfortunate woman this morning and I am now clear that the scoundrel Paxton had come to her with stories of the unsuitability of the local bank manager. He had asked her to encourage her husband to talk to the clerk about the change of accounts so that he could claim that the initiative came from the clergyman. Mrs. Russell has had a hard time of it these last few years, but I believe she is a strong enough woman to recover from this tragedy."

"Once we arrived in the city I asked Watson to investigate the disappearance of Miss Black. His information persuaded me that she was engaged to someone, that she probably believed him to be the Revd. Russell and was innocent of the real nature of the matter in which she was involved. Her note was clearly written for her and the fact that it mentioned the reverend gentleman by name, made me suspect that it was written by someone intending to incriminate him, rather than the Revd. Russell himself. The fact that it mentioned financial arrangements again pointed towards the parish clerk."

"This brings us to Bennett or Paxton himself. For those who do not know the background to the case, Paxton came from a good family and was trained in accounting, but gambling brought him down. He ran up huge debts and he solved them by stealing from his clients. These included two clergymen whom he attempted, separately, to defraud. When they realised the crime that was being committed he cold-bloodedly murdered them. He was eventually tracked down in London, where I know Lestrade was involved in escorting the man back to Lincoln to face the hanging judge."

"Very right Mr. Holmes," said Lestrade. "I'll never forget that character. He was as clever as they come and a fine actor. All the way back to Lincoln he maintained an air of complete calm, as if the murders were nothing whatsoever to do with him. As soon as I saw his face in the lamp last night I recognised him."

"I, however, had never seen Paxton," continued Holmes. "So I telegraphed Lincoln Prison to ask for any distinguishing features. They told me that he has a nasty scar caused by a burn on his right forearm. That, Watson, is why I was shaking his hand, examining the plans and asking to see the ledger. I wanted his sleeve to slip back and reveal the scar. It was only when he reached up to the top shelf for the accounts book that my suspicions were confirmed."

"We could, of course, have had him arrested there and then, but I wanted to try and persuade him to reveal the truth about the most recent murder. Hence the charade in the graveyard. But, I should have known Paxton better, he was too clever to be caught by a trap, we simply had to chase him down. It will be for you, Lestrade, to uncover the finer details of the case, such as how he secured the money from the unfortunate cleric." Holmes stretched out his long legs and reached for his pipe. "I think that covers everything gentlemen."

"What about Miss Black?" I asked.

"Quite right Watson. After seeing Mrs. Russell this morning, I visited the Dean to explain the outcome of the investigation. I have to say that he seemed more relieved that his cleric's reputation was unsullied than sad that the Revd. Russell was dead. He has offered to send a local clergyman, at the church's expense, to Paris to bring the poor Miss Black home to her family. I hope she is somewhat chastened by her experiences."

After a pause Holmes turned to me and said "So Watson, let us pack our bags and set off for London where we can turn our attention to the problems of Mr. Augustus Buckskin-Popham and his peculiarly complex fraud case."

ADVERTISEMENTS.

R. W. WHITTAKER,

FAMILY BAKER,

Pastrycook and Confectioner,

NEXT FALSTAFF HOTEL,

WESTGATE, CANTERBURY.

Tea, Coffee, Chocolate & Light Refreshments.

WEDDING CAKES A SPECIALITY.

W. E. GODDEN,

Hairdresser & Wigmaker,

51, Burgate Street.

CANTERBURY.

Ladies' Combings made up in any Style.

FEMALE ATTENDANT IF REQUIRED FOR LADIES.

The Sunleys of Canterbury

"I see you have succumbed to this fashion for stories of phantasms and ghouls, Watson," said Holmes. It was a grey and wet November afternoon. The wind was hurling the rain against the windows of our rooms in Baker Street. Holmes sat curled on a pyramid of cushions by the fire, a pile of papers at his feet. He was, ostensibly, seeking out one or two papers that Gregson had asked him to supply for the trial of a case in which both had been involved. In truth, he was sitting in that state of complete lethargy that only he could achieve. This was Holmes the investigator without a case, the complete antithesis of the man of action I knew so well. For my part, I was sitting by the window in an effort to shield my choice of reading from Holmes' scornful view.

"How in the name of all that is wonderful can you divine my reading matter when I have taken such care to hide it from you?" I replied with a resigned laugh.

"It is precisely because you took such pains that I knew what you what you were reading. If you wish it, I will even tell you the title, author and publisher."

"Oh come Holmes, I know you are aware of my penchant for tales of the fantastic but I have taken great pains not to reveal the cover of this book to you."

"The book is *The Watcher*. The author is Le Fanu and the publisher is Downey and Co." I tossed the book to Holmes, who happily confirmed his theory. "If you wish to conceal your choice of reading matter from me you must be careful not to tear the announcement of the book's publication from the morning paper, shortly after I have read it. You must take equal care not to go immediately out for a stroll in a direction which will take you past Patterson's Bookshop and not to return with a carefully wrapped volume tucked under your arm."

I laughed at the simplicity of the explanation for a feat which had so confounded me.

"But surely you see no harm in reading such stories?" I asked. "It is not as if they are to be believed."

"I would have thought," replied my friend, "that it is the germ of suspicion that such spectres might exist that gives these tales the frisson you seem to so enjoy. However, read them if you wish but leave me to the more terrifying prospect of the crimes of our fellow men." We lapsed into silence and Holmes stood up and began pacing the room until he stopped by the window through which he stared miserably at the falling rain. "I would think only phantasms would make the effort to consult us on a day like this," he sighed after gazing out across the rooftops for many minutes. "No wait, I do believe a carriage is drawing up. Perhaps hope is at hand."

In reviewing the case of the Sunleys of Canterbury, that ghoulish preamble has always seemed peculiarly appropriate. In a sense Holmes and I found ourselves investigating ghosts, even if our client turned out to be made of very solid stuff. I joined my colleague at the window and looked down to see a man emerging from the carriage. He was caped in black with a large black hat balanced on his head. This garb so concealed him that all we could discern from this distance was that he was well below average height. The doorbell rang insistently and fortunately our housekeeper moved swiftly to allow the caller in out of the rain. I had already turned away from the window in expectation of our visitor, but Holmes continued to stare down at the cab as if some particular point had caught his interest. "What is it that has so attracted your attention Holmes?" I asked.

"A mere detail Watson. I was simple trying to determine from which part of America this fellow originates." I laughed at the audacity of Holmes' comment, but he waved away my inquiries, saying simply "Let us hope that he brings us some challenge to drive out all thought of this depressing day."

Mrs. Hudson pushed open the door and announced a Mr. Henry Sunley. Deprived of his hat and cape he appeared even smaller than our first impression. He could have been very little over five feet tall, but he had a powerful build with broad shoulders and a thick, muscular neck. His hair was a cropped grey, but still showed hints of the fiery colour that it must have been in his youth. I put his age at anywhere between fifty and sixty. His face was red and swarthy as if he was used to the outdoor life but his clothes appeared to be of a good cut although somewhat dishevelled.

"Welcome Mr. Sunley," said Holmes with enthusiasm. "I see you have very recently arrived from New York."

"By heavens Mr. Holmes, it appears that everything they say about you is true. I stepped off the boat this very lunchtime and have come here to Baker Street without a moment's hesitation."

"Then I am sure that you would welcome some English hospitality. Watson, a whisky for our guest."

"That's mighty kind of you sir," said Sunley in a very definite American drawl. "Would it be foolish to ask how you knew of my origins before I even opened my mouth."

"Elementary details," he replied. "The luggage on the cab, the cut of your cape and hat, the state of your clothes, all were indicative. More important is the question of what brings you to our door with such haste."

Our visitor sat himself by the fire and took a sip of the whisky I had handed him and then began to unfold the situation in a clear but thoughtful manner. "I am here because six months ago a correspondent in London sent me the following extract clipped from one of your daily papers." He pulled out his pocket book and handed us a small corner of newsprint. "As you can see, it reports a dreadful accident that occurred outside the Buffs Barracks in Canterbury. It tells how a munitions waggon carrying a large quantity of explosives had detonated on its journey to Canterbury. Three men had died. One of them was named as a Lieutenant Albert Sunley of Canterbury."

For a moment I thought of the horrific accidents involving explosives that I had seen during my brief period in the army. The lucky ones were those who died instantly, the unfortunates were left as twisted imitations of their former selves, condemned to live a half life full of others' pity and revulsion.

"I assume," said Holmes returning me to the matter in hand, "that Lieutenant Sunley was a relative of yours."

"Yes, I believe that he would have been my cousin twice removed. However, you must appreciate that, for reasons that I will explain shortly, the American and British sides of the family have been at odds for the last two generations. I do not, therefore, feel this tragedy as a personal loss. Yet it has made me determined to resolve the animosity between the two halves of the family."

"Your motives seem very noble, but I do not understand how I might be of service," said Holmes. "I cannot imagine you wish me to investigate the circumstances around this tragic accident."

"Indeed not," returned Sunley. "I wish to consult you over a very particular matter which must be addressed before the family can be at peace once more. I must tell you that this case is somewhat out of the ordinary, and once I have explained it to you, I will understand if you choose to reject my commission."

"I would like nothing better than a case which is somewhat out of the ordinary, as you put it," laughed Holmes. "Please proceed."

"Mr. Holmes," said the American, "I wish you to investigate a murder."

"I would be only too happy to oblige," said Holmes with genuine enthusiasm, "but, I would be hard pressed to investigate something that occurred at a distance of three thousand miles."

"No, it is somewhat less and somewhat more complex than that. The murder, if such it was, took place in Canterbury," said Sunley obscurely.

"You surprise me, Mr. Sunley, I scan the papers with great care and was not aware of any recent unsolved tragedies in Kent," replied Holmes.

Sunley laughed. "That is the point Mr. Holmes, the events to which I allude took place about 80 years ago."

"You interest me even more," said Holmes.

"My great-grandfather," he began, "was a wealthy landowner in Kent. He had a large estate on the road from Whitstable to Canterbury at a place called Blean. William Sunley was his name and he was known as a very devout and religious man. He was a widower with two grown, but as yet unmarried, sons. Both lads, Herbert and George, lived in the large house on the estate but you could not find two more different people. Herbert was a wild one, taken to gambling and the high life. George followed the religious inclinations of his father and was considering seeking ordination."

"Nonetheless, it is said that the three men lived tolerably well together. Until, that is, the 6th day of October 1818." He paused to draw breath, which added a dramatic effect to his next statement. "On that day their father disappeared, never to be seen again. A note was found in his handwriting on a scrap of paper saying that he had gone away to convert to the Roman Catholic church and intended to spend the rest of his days as a religious. There is no other evidence as to what happened to him. No trace of him was ever found. Enquiries were made of various churches and monasteries on the continent, but nothing was ever discovered."

"Following this, the father's will was found which left, as was usual I understand, the bulk of the land to the elder son Herbert. George was to receive a very small income. Yet, the father was not known to be dead, so it was uncertain whether the will should be enforced. Despite that, Herbert, knowing that one day he would inherit, began to act as if he were the lord of the manor, so to speak. He started selling off outlying fields to pay debts, dismissing members of the staff if they offended him, and above all refusing to support George in his desire to enter university or seek ordination. Herbert might spend his inheritance but he refused to allow George, whom he treated abysmally, to touch the income that was his by right. In the end, it seems that George, seeing no prospects of a satisfactory conclusion to his

Advertisements.

A. BATES,
Gun and Cycle Maker,
22, SUN ST., CANTERBURY.

HAMMERLESS GUNS FROM £5 TO £50.

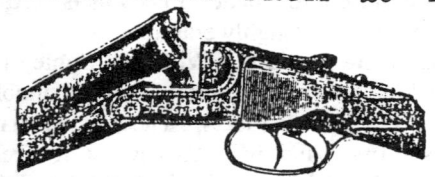

THE FARMER'S GUN, Double Breech Loader, Rebounding Locks, £2 10s.
Converted Shot Rifles for long distance Shooting, made from Government Rifles, 15s. and 17s. 6d. each.

GUNS LENT ON HIRE.
Over 500 acres good Mixed Shooting to let by day or longer.

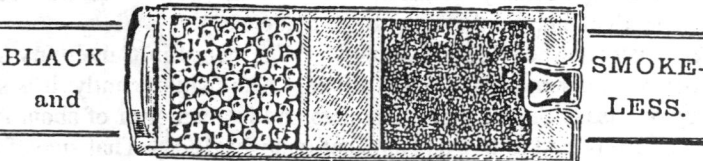

BLACK and — SMOKE-LESS.

Cartridges 6/-, 8/6, and 10/- per 100.

CYCLES, ALL HIGH GRADE — MACHINES KEPT IN STOCK.

Machines may be purchased on the easy terms.
CYCLES on HIRE by the HOUR, DAY or WEEK.

affairs, decided to join a boat making for America and to start a new life out there. Thus, my father and myself were born on that great continent."

"What you have said is all very clear," said Holmes. "But where is the murder?"

"It has been a firmly held belief on my side of the family that Herbert Sunley murdered his father and thus deprived George of his birthright," replied our visitor in the straightforward manner which I was beginning to recognise as characteristic of this American.

Holmes pursed his lips and thought for a moment, tapping his long fingers together in time to a rhythm that only he could hear. "Your case is undoubtedly intriguing," he said, "but without evidence what can I investigate? I cannot inquire into a belief, I need facts. At this distance in time all traces will have been thoroughly erased."

"But Mr. Holmes, there are facts." With that Sunley reached into his coat and pulled out a long brown envelope. From it tumbled a variety of folded slips of paper. "These are the facts. These papers have been handed down from father to son in my family. All have been carefully preserved, occasionally even in the face of fire or flood, in the hope that one day the justice of George Herbert's case would be proven." He placed them on the floor at Holmes' feet like some offering. My friend fell on them with delight and spent upwards of half an hour turning the documents over, examining the paper and peering carefully at the handwriting.

"They are undoubtedly genuine," he said at last. "It will be a challenge to study them. Is there any more evidence?"

"There may well be," replied Sunley. "The house in Canterbury still stands, albeit with a somewhat smaller estate. More significantly, it is still occupied by one Isaac Sunley who I understand is a widower of about fifty years of age. He is said to live a somewhat reclusive life. That side of the family has had little fortune. I am told that one relative fell in the Sutlej campaign in the Crimea and now his only child has been killed in this ghastly accident. It is possible that his side of the family and indeed the house itself might reveal some further evidence."

"Very possibly," said Holmes thoughtfully. "Have you contacted him at all?"

"I wrote him a letter a while back when I heard of his son's death, but never received a word in reply. I guess he thinks I am a kind of crackpot or some such. Do you have any suggestions Mr Holmes?" asked Sunley.

"There are undoubtedly a number of ways to handle that aspect of this affair. However, before I proceed in this matter it is essential that I ask you one further question." Holmes paused as if choosing his words carefully. "If

I prove that your grandfather was cheated of his inheritance will you claim the estate for yourself?"

Once again our visitor proved most direct. "So far I have told you nothing of my personal circumstances. It is true that George, my grandfather, started with nothing except his muscles and a few guineas, but over successive generations the Sunley family has worked hard and made the most of those limited resources. Thus, you are now looking at one of the Chicago meat kings. In London I may cut a somewhat inconsequential figure but in the stockyards of that growing city I am a man to be reckoned with. As a result I am also extremely wealthy. I have no doubt that, if I chose, I could buy the Canterbury estate several times over without missing the money for a moment. I am here," he continued with vigour, "to re-unite the two sides of the Sunley family. But my side of the family will always be reluctant to simply shake hands with our cousins unless every effort has been made to determine whether Herbert Sunley murdered his father and drove away his brother."

"So you will make no claim on any part of the estate, nor seek to deprive any relative of yours, no matter how distant, of their home, liberty or livelihood?"

"I give you my word, and would gladly sign a paper to that effect if it will persuade you to undertake this investigation."

"That will not be necessary" said Holmes. He rose and shook Sunley by the hand, his tall, spare frame contrasting sharply with the short, stocky figure before him. "I will accept your word as a gentleman. Watson here will be our witness." I nodded my assent and moved to shake Sunley by the hand. Holmes, however, was already bustling about preparing to examine the secrets of the documents Sunley had provided. "Come Watson help me move these papers to the table and then bring the lamp. We will need light to decipher some of these old scripts."

The three of us had to shuffle around moving the piles of documents that littered every surface and finding pens and pads for note taking before Holmes could settle down to his task. I had rarely seen him so enthused for an investigation. Sunley, however, felt the need to return our attention to more mundane matters. "I am sorry to have to raise such questions Mr. Holmes but, as you observed, I came straight here from the boat and have yet to claim my bed at the hotel. Perhaps you could excuse me for a while so that I can settle into my suite." The American spoke in a manner which clearly acknowledged that Holmes was now the master in this affair.

"Out of the question," replied Holmes directly. "I need you here to help me interpret these texts. I cannot spare you. Watson, make our guest a bed on the sofa and then call down to Mrs. Hudson for coffee and a hot meal for yourselves. I will take nothing thank you."

Sunley turned to me with a chuckle. "It is many a year since I slept in anything other than a full size bed, but I have a feeling that this evening will be well worth a small amount of discomfort. I gladly accept your hospitality."

Thus began an evening that neither Sunley nor I will ever forget. Outside the wind continued to drive the rain against our window panes, but inside we were transported back to the beginning of the century. For several hours Holmes examined the documents in great detail. He would peer at them through a lens, hold them up to the light, decipher the text and make notes on the pad at his elbow. From time to time he would turn to Sunley and ask for his opinion on a particular point touching the family history. But for most of the evening Sunley and I sat by the fire, swapping stories about our youthful adventures in hushed tones, and as the night grew later we dozed fitfully while Holmes devoured the papers. Then, as the clock chimed a quarter before two in the morning, Holmes pushed back his chair and said "Well gentlemen, it would assist me greatly if you would act as my audience while I run through the picture of events that has emerged from these papers."

There was not a trace of fatigue in his voice or demeanour. As I have often remarked, when Holmes is on a case he seems to call upon wellsprings of energy which were certainly denied to Sunley and myself. We pulled ourselves out of the stupor which the fire and the occasional brandy had encouraged and readied ourselves to listen to Holmes' account.

"Here is our starting point," my friend began, selecting a long strip of newsprint from the pile at his side. "I am sure you will be familiar with the contents of this paragraph Mr. Sunley, but for Watson's benefit I will summarise it. This has been drawn from the Kentish Gazette for the 10th day of October 1818. It relates general concerns about the disappearance of William Sunley. It confirms that he had left a note suggesting that he was seeking the contemplative life, but expresses anxiety that no-one saw him leave. According to this excellent reporter, the day in question was a Sunday, Mr. Sunley had been seen at church for matins and then again with his two sons later for the main morning service which was a harvest celebration. We are told that he was in fine spirits. All three returned home to host an "amusement" that the family held annually in their gardens for all the estate workers. By four o'clock that afternoon he had disappeared taking only a small leather bag and some clothes."

Holmes put the paper to one side and picked up a second, hand written, paper. "This is a letter from a friend of your grandfather. He seems to have been present at the amusement and confirms many of the points in the newspaper article. He adds the significant detail, that the grounds of the house were very busy at all times, so it was difficult to see how William Sunley could have left without being observed."

Holmes then turned to a small leatherbound notebook. "This is the first volume of the journal that George Sunley kept on his voyage to America. I have read it at speed and can find only one significant reference, but it is the most suggestive. The journal opens thus *My father has been murdered and I am fleeing. There will be no justice for that poor sweet man. It is cowardice that prevents me from doing right. I must turn my back on that past. I can look only to the future now. That past life died with my slaughtered father. May God have mercy on his soul.*

I made to comment on what appeared to be very damning evidence, but Holmes was determined to pursue his presentation of the facts. "This, Mr. Sunley, is your great grandfather's will. As you suggested, it gives the bulk of the estate to his first born son. My first interest, however, has not been in the content but rather the signature. You will, no doubt, both be aware that the study of handwriting is now a considerable science and one of which I have made a special study. The manner in which a document is written can reveal a great deal about its author and his state of mind. This will was of little help in revealing anything specific about your great grandfather. It has clearly been drawn up by a solicitor and copied out by his clerk, but the signature here is that of a much older man than the main body of the will." He waved the will in our direction before casting it to one side. He then drew out a small ragged scrap of paper and held it very carefully so that we could see its exact dimensions.

"Here we have the note that was found on his disappearance. This I believe is in his own hand. I have examined the note and compared it with the signature on the will and I am convinced they are one and the same. There is, more importantly, no sign of mental agitation in the writing. These words were not penned under duress. The conclusion is that your forebear voluntarily wrote that he intended to leave for a contemplative life."

"You disappoint me Mr. Holmes, that letter has always seemed to be a particular stumbling block to my family's opinion that Herbert murdered his father and now you are confirming that it is genuine." Holmes held up his hand and prevented Sunley from continuing.

"In this case, the significance of the paper is not its content but rather that it has been torn. There are two significant points which can be learnt from these tears, but at present I will only refer you to one of them. This paper has been torn from a larger document. A close examination reveals that there are signs of other letters above and below this fragment of text. This paragraph has been literally ripped from its context. My belief is that your great-grandfather did write of his intention to pursue the contemplative life, but that it was hedged around with other conditions. An unknown hand has wrenched out that suggestion to make it appear like a note of farewell."

"Excellent Mr. Holmes, the case against Herbert seems to be slowly developing," said Sunley with unmistakable delight.

"It would be a capital error for any competent investigator to draw such a conclusion. All that we have said is all that we can say with certainty." Sunley took the correction in good part and my colleague continued with his account. "My final step was to try and identify the different hands of the two brothers. George's was simple to confirm as it is here in the journal. Your grandfather has most fortuitously also left us a couple of bills of sale for horses and other farm animals. These contain clear example of his brother's hand," said Holmes holding up a document relating to the purchase of a small number of cows. " I hope you will note its peculiar features and here at the foot of the page is his signature."

We nodded sagely, but I doubt if either Sunley or I could read one hundredth part of what Holmes could discern. "These few documents persuade me that there is good reason to believe that William Sunley was murdered. The entry in the journal, the strange disappearance at a time when the house was surrounded by people, and particularly the note which was torn out of a larger document, all point in that direction. If he was leaving of his own volition, would he not leave more than a torn scrap of paper?"

Holmes now held us in his thrall, as he had so many people in the past, while he wove impossible pictures from the slimmest of threads. "The evidence also points to the fact that he was killed by someone close to him. This murder must have been perpetrated on the spur of the moment, no-one would choose the busiest day of the year on which to undertake such an act. But on the spur of the moment a stranger would not have known that the note in question existed or where it could be found. There are a number of other facts with which I will not detain you at the moment."

"So what is your next step Mr. Holmes?" asked Sunley.

"Our next step is to snatch what rest we can and then take the train to Canterbury."

The next morning, we were to have left by the Charing Cross train to Canterbury West, but flooding had caused a landslip and we were forced to travel on the London Chatham and Dover line out of Victoria to the East station. As a result, the train was crowded and we found ourselves travelling with a group of amateur photographers in their bowler hats and loaded down with boxes and bags full of equipment. They chattered noisily about the prospects of finding sufficient light to capture the cathedral, until Holmes engaged them in an absorbing conversation about the uses of photography in criminal investigations. Sunley, however, spent the journey peering out excitedly at the English countryside, while I dozed quietly in the corner of the carriage.

Canterbury is always prone to flooding, at worst the Stour will burst its bank and inundate the High Street. So we were relieved to find that the storms of the last couple of days had not had such calamitous results, but the roads were still more like ponds than pathways and were thick with mud. We took a carriage to a convenient inn to leave our bags and then set off for Blean. At Holmes' insistence Sunley did not accompany us on the first stage of the investigation. "Your presence will rouse too many prejudices at this initial encounter." Sunley protested, but sensed he was in the presence of a man who would brook no disagreement and demurred.

The road to Whitstable leads up the steep, bleak hill that overlooks the city to the west. We rode out through the Westgate and past some of the ancient inns and churches of this beautiful city. Then the carriage climbed slowly up the steep and slippery hill until it finally breasted the summit and ran the short way down into the village of Blean.

The Sunley estate was hidden by high hedges and red brick walls just past the village. The house itself was approached by a short gravelled drive which opened up, somewhat after the French fashion, into a large arc in front of the house with enough standing for several carriages. At the centre of this expanse was an old, and sadly no longer functional, fountain complete with spouting dolphins covered with a thick green patina. The house itself was a dark construction of flint and brick with the year 1730 chiselled above the entrance. Although this scene was pleasant enough, it was not the house, the driveway or the fountain that caught our eye.

Our attention was riveted rather, on a tall dark haired figure bicycling round and round the fountain in great ellipses on one of the increasingly rare Royal Salvo Tricycles. These it will be recalled had two large wheels on either side of the rider and the one small wheel in front. He steered this contraption by means of the two handles beside his knees which made him appear like nothing less than an ape on wheels. He was watched by a pretty young maid who was laughing fit to burst at these antics.

The cyclist and the girl became aware of our gaze at the same instant. The former immediately dismounted and the maid disappeared around the side of the house. The man straightened his clothes and then walked slowly over to see us. He was tall and dark with an appearance that suggested he was constantly at odds with the world. My immediate reaction was that this was not a gentleman, or at least not one that I would care to trust. However, he was well dressed in a pair of grey tweeds.

"Good morning gentlemen," he said stiffly. "Can I help you?"

"Mr. Isaac Sunley?" asked Holmes clearly aware that this figure did not tally with the Isaac Sunley we had been expecting to meet. The tall man shook his head. "My name is Harrison, I am Mr. Sunley's secretary."

"I am Sherlock Holmes and this is my friend and colleague Dr. Watson."

Harrison seemed to be struggling to recollect where he had heard that name before. "What can I do to help you gentlemen?" he inquired.

"I have been commissioned by Mr. Henry Sunley of Chicago..." Holmes had said little more when a sudden change came over the sombre figure before us.

"No! Mr. Sunley will not see you!" He seemed to realise that he was shouting so he collected himself and continued more calmly. "I have strict instructions to have nothing to do with this impostor Sunley and his fraudulent claims. I bid you good morning gentlemen."

It seemed to me that we had arrived at an impasse. Our plans depended on Mr Isaac Sunley being willing to help us to advance the investigation. If he would not co-operate we could do little, and I doubted that this was a case that merited more illicit means of looking at the evidence within the house. At that moment, fortunately, the deadlock was broken and we secured entry to the house in a most unexpected manner.

A tall stooping figure with long wispy grey hair and a pallid appearance appeared at the top of the steps into the house. I have always been of the view that the outward appearance of a man is a sure indicator of the state of the inward man. If that is the case then Mr. Sunley was an all but empty vessel. He appeared desiccated like a withered seed pod. His brown tweeds added to the impression of decay. They may have been similar in age and have been distantly related but it was hard to find a pair of people less alike than the two Sunleys.

"What do these gentlemen want, Harrison?" asked the old man in a thin voice.

"It is nothing, sir. They are just leaving," replied the secretary.

"I am Sherlock Holmes and this is my friend and colleague Dr. Watson. I have been commissioned by Mr. Henry Sunley of Chicago..." Holmes repeated the introduction he had given to Harrison and again it had a startling effect. The old man let out a groan of profound agony, turned an almost greenish hue and then collapsed in a feint onto the ground.

"Help me Watson," said Holmes running towards the crumpled figure and scooping him up in his arms. Between the two of us, we carried the surprisingly light figure up the short flight of stone steps into the darkened interior of the house. Once inside, we were dismayed at the vision of decay all around us. The place was ill-lit, so it was difficult to discern the details but the carpet was shabby, parts of the wall seemed to be peeling away and pictures, mirrors and virtually every other visible surface were covered with a thick layer of grime.

Harrison followed us at our heels, protesting continually that we should not have come, that he had warned us away, and that we would end up killing his master with such news. We took Sunley into a stale smelling drawing room, placed him on a grey and tattered chaise longue and I set about loosening his collar, feeling for his pulse and attempting to revive him. Harrison stood at my elbow and said "I thank you gentlemen for your assistance, but I am quite able to handle this matter now. My master would appreciate it if you left."

I turned on my heels and faced the secretary. "I am a doctor, Harrison. I have taken certain oaths and I will not abandon a man who may be in need of my help without at least examining him and reassuring myself of his well-being." I spoke in my sternest manner, although I was still uncertain of the rectitude of this course of action.

"Stout fellow, Watson," muttered Holmes.

On a table near to hand was a carafe of water and a glass. I gestured to Holmes to pour some for my patient. Harrison again tried to intervene, protesting that it was not fresh and that he would find him some recently drawn water. Holmes, however, had already bent to pour the drink. I saw him pause and then stand up, with the glass in his hand. "Perhaps, Harrison, you could find your master some brandy or some such reviving liquor instead," Holmes said in a commanding tone.

Harrison nodded, as he left he tried to pick up the water carafe, but Holmes stood squarely in his way and said "Do hurry Harrison." Once he had departed, Holmes grasped the glass of water and sniffed it.

"We will not be using this Watson," he said offering me the glass. "Smell it."

There was an undoubted bitter aroma about the water.

"It is poisoned," said Holmes simply.

"We seem to have stumbled from an old mystery into a present mystery," I said.

"Do you think so, Watson? I would have thought that there was very little mystery about this at all. No matter, attend to your patient and I will attend to my investigations." As I administered the brandy, Holmes prowled around the room examining books and peering at ancestral portraits. At last Sunley sat up and peered at us with a look of profound anxiety.

"Mr. Holmes, this is a disaster. You have come here to destroy me, I know it." He blurted his words out with a weak but desperate force. "You see what I am brought to, this once proud family home is crumbling around me and now you want to steal that from me as well. You are witnesses to the delicacy of my health. What should become of me if I had to leave here. The workhouse, that would be my destination. I will finish my days in the workhouse with young Harrison here, my trusty servant. All because some rapacious American who bears my name and claims my kinship wants to steal this house on some pretence that my ancestor was a murderer. It is not right Mr. Holmes. It is not right."

He threatened to continue in this vein until all his energies were spent. So I moved across to him and put a reassuring hand on his arm, and tried to tell him that his fears were groundless. He began to sob quietly like a little child. After a while he calmed sufficiently for Holmes to begin to try and explain the facts of the situation. He told him about the assurance that Henry Sunley had given that he would make no claim on the Canterbury property, and that his only interest was in clearing up a family mystery. He explained the nature of the investigation to date and how we would be keen to discuss the matter with the English side of the family and examine the scene of the alleged murder. "You will surely not deny your cousin this?" concluded Holmes in his most appealing manner.

"He wrote to me, you know. I was convinced that he was here simply to steal my property and claim the house. You must excuse my excitable nature but I am not a well man. Ever since I received the letter I have been dreading this moment." He picked up the brandy glass and took a few fortifying sips while we waited for him to speak. "As I say I view this encounter with trepidation, but if you provide me with a written undertaking from Mr. Sunley that he will not make a claim, however this affair should fall out, then I will entertain you gentlemen and my relative tomorrow at this hour."

ADVERTISEMENTS.

'OZO' — STOPS HEADACHE. — **'OZO'**
CURES NEURALGIA.
'OZO' — CURES INFLUENZA. — **'OZO'**
STOPS TOOTHACHE.

And all RHEUMATIC NERVE PAINS in a FEW MINUTES.

It is TASTELESS & EASILY SWALLOWED.

→ 8 Doses for 6½d. ←

From the Inventors and Manufacturers—

WALKER & HARRIS,

THE CHEAPEST CHEMISTS IN KENT,

CANTERBURY,

ASHFORD, AND RAMSGATE.

SEND FOR PRICE LIST.

I had been watching Harrison throughout the interview, and noticed that he was becoming more and more agitated. At last he spoke. "Master, I must, respectfully, remind you that this is a most dangerous course of action. We should have nothing to do with these men. You are admitting a viper into our midst." His words were urgent and betrayed a profound anxiety.

"You are right to be concerned for me Harrison," said the old man kindly. "But I will meet my cousin. It will be painful, but perhaps family duty demands it." He stood up to see us out of his house, but as he did so he collapsed into a second feint. Such was his state that we had to carry him to his room and I sent the girl we had seen in the grounds, who seemed to be a young kitchen skivvy, into the city to buy chloral as a nerve tonic.

"I fear that he is not a well man," I said to Holmes. "It is my duty to stay here a while until he shows some signs of recovery. I would not want to feel responsible for delivering such a blow that we sent a man to his grave from the fright."

"A capital idea," said Holmes. "We shall both stay here and pursue our chosen calling. You will act as his doctor while I examine the house and gardens."

Sunley's room had a stale, neglected air. It put me in mind of nothing so much as Mr. Dickens' descriptions of Ebeneezer Scrooge's bedchamber. There was an old four poster with curtains which were long past their best. The sheets and blankets were grey and neglected. The fireplace stood cold and empty even at this late stage of the year. I checked my patient again and then settled myself into a dusty winged chair, which I turned so that I could see both the bed and command a view of a most attractive garden.

The back of the house appeared to open onto a veranda and then immediately onto a lawn, which in the summer would have been beautifully shaded by a long screen of lime trees. To the right was the ivy clad wall of a kitchen garden and beyond it could be seen a church tower. In other circumstances it would have been a charming picture, indeed one scarcely to be equalled, and certainly not exceeded, in any other village in Kent.

I, however, found myself enduring a long and tedious vigil. For two hours I sat in that room. My only entertainment was an occasional glimpse of Holmes prowling through the garden. At one point he seemed to be circling the house ceaselessly. I counted at least six circuits, each time he would be peering about him, staring up at the house or examining the layout of the garden. As the afternoon wore on I heard Holmes' impatient footsteps moving around the various floors of the house. Feeling confident that Sunley would suffer no further relapses, I left him alone and went in search of my colleague. I found him crouching on the floor of what must once have been a splendid library, but which was now a rather shabby and dusty room, with large spaces on the shelves where I imagine books had been sold to raise much needed funds. Holmes' only interest seemed to be the state of the floorboards. "Watson!" he said with his eyes still fixed on the floor. "How is the patient?"

"He is sleeping soundly, I have no doubt that he will recover from this shock. Have you discovered anything?"

"I have learnt only a little in the last two hours. Up to a certain point I am very clear of the facts of the case. I feel, however, that the situation here could reach a crisis very shortly. I have no doubt that since the death of his master's only son, Harrison has had his eye on a share of the inheritance from the estate. He may even have been promised such a prize. He is, therefore, opposed to anything that will reunite the family and so disinherit himself. I also fear that he is using poison to slowly weaken his master's constitution to a point where that inheritance may not be long denied him."

"This is terrible!" I exclaimed. "We must act at once!"

"Indeed we must, but I also wish to bring the other half of this investigation to a satisfactory conclusion. Are you willing to play a wild gamble with me Watson?" He peered out of the window at the gathering clouds. "It may mean a wet, cold and ultimately futile evening."

"Have I ever failed you before?" I asked.

"Never," he replied. "Let us bait the trap then." He went to the top of the stairs and called for Harrison who came swiftly up to join us.

"We must leave now," said Holmes, to the secretary's evident relief. "Doctor Watson feels that your master will sleep soundly now for many hours under the influence of the nerve tonic. We will see you in the morning."

As we descended the stairs Harrison asked with feigned disinterest "Have you discovered anything which sheds light on the disappearance of William Sunley?"

"Oh yes!" said Holmes with real enthusiasm. "I have discovered evidence which touches, if you like, the very bones of the matter. Tomorrow morning I will reveal all."

Harrison looked very uncomfortable at that news and bid us a rather curt farewell. As we walked swiftly back towards the city Holmes said "That was a very long shot, and a rather crude one at that, but if there is any evidence to be found I rather think Harrison will be moved to ensure we fail to find it tomorrow. But for now we must hurry back to our American friend and secure his assistance this evening."

Holmes and I splashed our way back through the sodden lanes into the city. Henry Sunley was sitting in the inn enjoying his first taste of English ale by an English fire. It was a welcoming sight after the decay of the old house, but the American was keen to hear all our news. "I can't deny this is a beautiful place Mr Holmes, but I haven't really had the stomach for seeing the sights. All I could think about was the progress of your investigations. I demand to know every detail of your afternoon," said Sunley with enthusiasm.

"Patience, Watson and I are soaked to the very marrow. You must allow us to dry out and change our clothes. I am afraid, however, that there will be no rest for any of us. Once changed we have work to do, if you will join us."

"With pleasure, Mr. Holmes," said the American ignorant of what was to come.

It was dark by four o'clock and with dusk came more torrential rain, but Holmes would not be deterred. We walked the two or three miles back to the house across muddy fields and along lanes awash with streams of filthy water "I have set the trap and I must be there to seize whatever we catch," he declared. That was to mean a cold damp evening for the three of us.

Holmes had discovered that Harrison lived in a small cottage about one hundred yards from the back of the house. After stealthily checking that the secretary was at home, Holmes chose a small wood store for our vantage point, it being the only place to offer a modicum of shelter along with a view of the cottage. For six long hours, Holmes, Sunley and I sat silently waiting for Harrison to emerge and lead us wherever he might. There were many moments when I wanted nothing more than to abandon the whole enterprise. As water forced its way down the back of my collar and dribbled coldly down my spine, I dreamt of coffee, of sandwiches and of hot meat pies. All we had was the occasional drop of brandy from my hip flask. Holmes remained resolute throughout. He scarcely moved, and his gaze remained concentrated on the cottage as if his life depended on it. What our American friend made of it, I could only guess.

Towards eleven o'clock the rain ceased, a cool wind blew the clouds apart and a half moon threw a brilliant light onto the dark garden. At that moment we heard the scrape and click of a key turning in a lock. Across the lawn we saw the tall dark figure of Harrison emerge from the cottage.

He glanced swiftly around him and then set off into the trees that led away from the house.

Holmes bounded silently from our hiding place and beckoned us to follow him. We could see Harrison in the moonlight moving purposefully ahead, oblivious to the train he was dragging behind him. We had to tread carefully and avoid the crack of sticks or splashing in the many puddles along the way. The walk was, however, to be relatively brief. Harrison turned into a field and made for a hayloft which stood at the end of it. On an instinct, I bent down and picked up a solid stick which I spotted lying by the side of the path. None of us had come armed and I felt the better for some means of defence. Harrison had stopped at the door of the loft and lit a lamp that he had been carrying under his cloak. He then put a key to a padlock and disappeared inside. I was amused to note the words "TEMPERANCE 1802" in stone above the lintel.

"We will leave him five minutes and then go in," said Holmes. We stood silently in the shadow of a tree and strained to hear the sounds emerging from the loft. Footsteps crossed a wooden floor. Objects were moved about and then a brief pause was followed by the sound of planks being levered up.

"The moment has come," said Holmes. He strode forward, opened the door and dashed into the barn with Sunley and I close on his heels. Harrison was in the far corner bending over a hole in the floor. He was so engrossed in his task that he was oblivious to us until Holmes spoke. "Good evening, Mr. Harrison."

The servant swung round, in his hand was a jemmy he was using to raise the boards. In an instant he let out a vile curse and rushed towards us. As he raised the metal bar, I stepped to one side and struck him a hard blow on the shins with my stick and sent him tumbling across the floor. "Watson, once more I am in your debt," said my friend patting me on the shoulder in gratitude. "What would I do without you to look to my interests?" I burned with pleasure at the praise, but Holmes had already turned his attention to the prostrate figure at our feet.

"I've done nothing wrong Mr Holmes," he said in a wheedling voice. "I am only obeying my master's instructions."

"I believe that you have, as yet, done nothing for which a court could easily convict you, but your intentions are obvious to me. I doubt your motives are as innocent as you would have us believe," returned Holmes with asperity.

"Mr. Sunley, Mr. Isaac Sunley, knows that they are here. It has always been his intention to give them a decent Christian burial, but he always feared that the discovery of these... these things would cause a scandal."

"Wait a moment, Holmes," exclaimed Henry Sunley. "What are we talking of here? What have we found?"

"Mr. Sunley, under these floorboards are the mortal remains of your great-grandfather William Sunley," said Harrison simply.

"So he was murdered..." shouted the American with energy.

"Mr. Sunley," said Holmes in his most soothing voice, "you have been a sterling companion this evening. However, before we go any further I beg that Watson and yourself leave me here with Harrison so that I can conclude these investigations to my complete satisfaction. If we reassemble at the house at eleven o'clock tomorrow morning I will give you my final deductions."

Holmes' demeanour brooked no refusal. Sunley and I turned away and in the absence of any alternative, walked the couple of miles from Blean back to our hotel in the city. I recall on the way, the sight of the Cathedral from the hill above the town bathed in moonlight. The ancient edifice appeared to float in a soft mist above the city itself, so that it seemed impossible that men could have had a hand in such a creation. Sunley stood in wonder for many minutes at the handicraft of his ancestors. "I have seen so many amazing things today, Doctor, that if I could record them all no-one would believe me, but this is certainly the most beautiful." With that we walked on and down into the city and a welcome rest.

The next morning we took a carriage out to Isaac Sunley's house. As we splashed down the drive, I half expected to find Harrison out on his tricycle again, but was somewhat relieved to see the drive empty of anyone except the young girl who was sweeping the damp leaves into a pile. I left Sunley in the carriage and went into the house to find Holmes. I was pleased to see that Isaac Sunley was sitting up in his chair and talking brightly to my friend about the history of the estate.

"Dr Watson welcome!" he said climbing out of his chair and shaking me limply by the hand. "I must apologise for my outburst and sudden collapse yesterday. I am not at all myself at the moment. I am particularly grateful to you doctor for the care you extended to me. Is Mr Henry Sunley with you today?"

We nodded. "And do you have the paper you promised me yesterday?" he asked. Holmes handed him the document that I had prepared and Sunley read it several times with great attention. "I can find no fault in it, I suppose it would be proper to invite my cousin into the house." The three of us walked out to the carriage and I nodded that the American should come and join us. He leaped from the carriage with enthusiasm and strode up to his relative and shook him warmly by the hand.

"It is a great honour to meet you sir," he said genuinely. "I am grateful to you for extending me a welcome."

Isaac responded with little warmth saying only "I hope that you will feel your trip has been worthwhile." With that he led us back into his drawing room.

"I have spent the most fascinating night that I can recall in a very long time," said Holmes sitting down in a low chair and stretching his long legs before us.

"You look as fresh as if you had slept from dusk to dawn," I said noticing the healthy sheen to his usually pale cheeks.

"I would have thought that you could have recognised the invigorating transformation that a good investigation can work on the constitution," said Holmes with a laugh. "I must thank you, Mr. Sunley, for bringing such a remarkable case to my attention."

"I just hope that you have come to a clear conclusion," the American replied.

"I have indeed," said Holmes slowly.

"Well?" Henry Sunley was in a state of expectant agitation.

Holmes turned himself to face the American full on and said "I am certain, beyond reasonable doubt, that George Sunley murdered his father." There was a dumbfounded silence in the room.

"You mean Herbert do you not?" said the American in a bewildered tone.

"No," returned Holmes with great simplicity. "Your grandfather killed his own father with a knife blow to the ribs."

"Impossible!" Henry Sunley leapt from his chair seemingly on the edge of an explosive rage. The next few moments are the greatest testament to the personal qualities that America has bred into many of its sons. I watched for a moment wondering whether I would have to defend Holmes yet again. To my surprise and relief Sunley slumped back into his chair with a groan and put his head into his hands. He sat, sunk in deep contemplation for many minutes.

At last he looked up at Holmes and said "What you have said distresses me beyond measure, but I know that if you had said that Herbert was the murderer I would have believed you at once. I must, therefore, accept your verdict as willingly even if it runs against my own kin." He stood up and walked across the room. "Isaac Sunley, my family has done your family, no, our family, a great wrong. I hope you will take my hand and close for ever the rift that has lasted eighty years too long.

The old man was clearly much moved. He said nothing, but he willingly grasped the proffered hand and the two men embraced like long lost brothers. After a few moments of silence, the American said "I have accepted your verdict, Mr. Holmes, I ask now that you present your evidence."

"With pleasure," my friend replied. "My suspicions that we were pursuing the wrong brother were aroused in the very first moments of this case. I told you in my rooms in Baker Street that I was convinced that William Sunley was killed by someone who knew him intimately. The evidence of the note pointed to that. However, what you did not observe is that the note was torn by a left handed person. The handwriting of the two brothers showed Herbert to be right-handed, but George to be left-handed."

"Excellent! Magnificent!" cried the now animated Isaac Sunley who was clearly enjoying this exposition.

"As I told you last night," Holmes continued addressing Henry Sunley, "the bones of your great-grandfather lay in a long ignored cellar underneath the hayloft where we found Harrison last night. It is not possible to know how the body arrived there but it is most likely that the murder took place in the house, away from all the crowds but that George concealed the evidence when no-one would see him. On examining the body there was very clear evidence of a knife blow to the ribs. That blow was undoubtedly struck by a left-handed man."

"Thus to reconstruct the likely scene, while the estate workers amuse themselves on the lawns outside, father and son have a furious row about a subject which we will never divine. In a moment of rage, the usually passive George lashes out at his father and kills him. I have told you already that only an intimate of William Sunley could have known where to find the letter from which to abstract that parting note. His son would be one such person. He places the note where it will be found and then conceals the body somewhere in the house along with a small leather bag of clothes and effects. My deduction is that this was beneath the floor in the second bedroom to the left of the stairs. There is clear evidence of floorboards having been raised there many years ago, and my calculations suggest that the space beneath them could readily conceal a corpse. Once all is quiet he moves his father's remains to their current resting place."

At this point Isaac Sunley intervened to take up the story in his thin reedy voice. "That cellar door was long covered with old farm machinery. I suspect that George must have put it there to cover his crime. My father discovered the remains about thirty years ago. We realised immediately whose they were, but made the assumption that they were proof of the guilt of my grandfather. So we re-sealed the cellar and left them there. I have long wished to give them a Christian burial but the fear of stirring up a worse situation prevented me."

Henry Sunley had listened quietly to all that had been said. "I have one last question Mr. Holmes. How can you be sure that those are the bones of my great-grandfather?"

"I can offer you the most tangible proof. Beside his bones we found a small leather bag with his ancient effects, left there by his son eighty years ago. Here it is." He reached under his chair and proffered the American the very bag. Sunley opened it with reluctance and pulled out the rotting shirts and mouldy books within. As he fingered these most personal items I saw him begin to sob and I watched as shame for his grandfather convulsed his body. He buried his face into the shirt as those strong shoulders shook with sadness for all that had been lost.

"As to Harrison," said Holmes, "he has already fled."

"I had employed him since his youth," explained Isaac Sunley. "I had grown very fond of him. On the death of my son, I foolishly changed my will so that he would gain some benefit from the estate if I died. I even allowed him to use some of my son's clothes and that tricycle you saw him riding. Mr. Holmes has shown me how that trust was misplaced and I can see that my recent debilitation was largely caused by Harrison's subtle efforts to rid himself of me."

Holmes rose and said "My work is done here. Come Watson we must wish these gentlemen good day." With that we were off for a brief stroll through the Kent countryside and a train ride back to Holmes' beloved London.

I am happy to report, however, that this strange tale had a very pleasing coda. It is to Henry Sunley's credit that he did not immediately abandon his ancestral home and return to America. A sense of family loyalty encouraged him to freely help Isaac Sunley restore the Canterbury estates to their former glories. He asked nothing in return except the right to feel a certain pleasure at the restoration of his family pride. Many years later, we read with sadness of Isaac's death, but were pleased to learn that he had decided to leave the Canterbury estate to his American cousins, thus allowing the Sunley name to continue in the town. As Holmes said, when I told him about Isaac's dying wish, "It is reassuring to have been involved in at least one case from which good has clearly emerged triumphant."

ADVERTISEMENTS.

Hulbert & Son,

Satisfaction Guaranteed.

MUSIC PUBLISHERS AND SELLERS,
Professional Pianoforte Tuners & Repairers,

15, CASTLE STREET, CANTERBURY.

Dealers in Violins, Pianofortes, Harmoniums, American Organs, Music, &c.

Pianos for Sale, Hire, or Exchange.

FULL VALUE allowed for OLD PIANOS Taken in Exchange.

VIOLIN REPAIRS A SPECIALITY.

VIOLIN STRINGS AND FITTINGS. Dealers in old Violins, Harps, Bows, etc., etc.

Just Published, 'Valse Bohemienne,' by Cecil Gann.

THE MISSES GLOVER,
Indian and Oriental Art Stores,
52, ST. PETER'S STREET, CANTERBURY.

A variety of Quaint and Artistic Designs in Brass, Copper, Cloisonne, etc. SUITABLE FOR WEDDING AND BIRTHDAY GIFTS.

Condiments. Best Chutney and Curry bottled in India.

Sole Agents in Canterbury for "Aller Vale" Devonshire Pottery.

CARVED WOODWORK AND WICKERWORK.

Ladies' Cloak Room.

APARTMENTS, with or without Board.

AVENUE HOTEL, opposite Dane John Walk
(Near L.C.D. Rly. Station). CANTERBURY.

Phillips & Co.'s ALES & STOUT.
Wines, Spirits & Cigars.

LARGE BILLIARD ROOM.

Every Accommodation for Visitors.

Good Lock-up for Cycles.

Head-quarters of East Kent Quoit League.
Excellent Quoit Ground.
Private Entrance.

Chops, Steaks, Teas, at short notice.
COMFORTABLE BEDS.

Proprietor—**A. J. STEVENS.**

The Ball of Twine

It is strange to relate, but Mr. Sherlock Holmes often regarded those cases that were most acclaimed by the public as among his most significant failures. This has meant that a number of tales of particular interest have remained as notes in my casebook rather than as published accounts. Among these is the case that I have always thought of as the "Affair of the Ball of Twine."

In the last few weeks I have received a telegram from my friend's new home amidst the quiet lanes of Sussex. It seems that he has recently had correspondence with Stanley Hopkins, the promising young detective who, as you will no doubt be aware, has risen to great heights in the police force. Hopkins must have reminded him of this case because the message read "Publish twine now. Right that public know of my weaknesses. Holmes."

For my part, I have never regarded this case as a failure, like Hopkins and many others involved in it, particularly the poor widow Robbins whose vigilance initiated these circumstances, I believe it to be one of the foremost examples of Holmes' deductive powers.

It began one evening in the summer of 1895. Hopkins had, as was his occasional habit, called by our rooms in Baker Street to consult Holmes on an affair that was confounding the Kent Constabulary. The matter concerned two exceptionally brutal attacks that had occurred in Maidstone. One young man had been beaten to the very brink of death as he walked home from his office down a deserted alley. A week later another young man had been beaten to death in a very similar manner.

For over an hour Hopkins laid the facts before my friend. He had brought maps, photographs, and various reports all of which Holmes considered and then tossed to one side. At last he sighed and held up his hand. "Hopkins, you have delivered a more complete summary of the facts of a case than I have ever received from a police officer, so I am sorry that I will have to disappoint you. This is not a matter in which I can be of help. This is the province of an alienist, those doctors who specialise in afflictions of the psyche. These crimes are the work of a lunatic. As such it cannot be investigated by a mind that works on the principle of logic."

Hopkins attempted to protest but Holmes would not relent. We lapsed into silence as Hopkins packed away his papers and maps and then sat down to finish the whisky I had poured for him. "Do you have nothing that is more in my line?" asked Holmes eager for a new investigation.

"Not really, Mr. Holmes," he replied.

"*Not really* seems to suggest that there is something tucked away there, rather than nothing at all," my friend replied with a chuckle.

"As ever, you are right, there was a rather odd incident while I was at the Canterbury police station this afternoon, but I have to say that this seems to have more of madness about it than even the last case I mentioned," said Hopkins.

"Let me be the judge of that," said Holmes.

"As you wish. At about two o'clock this afternoon, an old widow, Mrs. Robbins by name, came bustling into the station in a state of great alarm. The constable on duty calmed her down and she began to explain that her house had been broken into by a burglar. There is, you will say, nothing extraordinary about that. What is unusual is that nothing was stolen. A window was forced open, a couple of her chairs had been moved around in her scullery and most surprisingly a brand new ball of twine had been left sitting on her kitchen table. There was no indication that the intruders had been disturbed and fled, they seemed to have come and gone of their own volition."

Holmes considered Hopkins' account for several minutes, and then asked "What action did you take?"

"The old lady was creating a considerable disturbance in the police station so a constable was dispatched to take her home and look at the broken window. There is not, however, a great deal that can be done. What would you suggest?"

"I would follow the string," said Holmes obscurely.

"Does that imply that you will investigate the matter, Holmes?" asked the policeman in surprise.

"No, it hardly seems to be of sufficient importance to merit a trip to Canterbury, but should anything else out of the ordinary happen to poor widow Robbins I will gladly come to your aid," said Holmes. "Now, I will take my violin and pipe and retire to my room. I bid you goodnight." With that Hopkins also took his leave and I followed Holmes' example and retired for the night, but my sleep was to be disturbed in a most unexpected manner.

At about four in the morning I awoke to find Holmes shaking my shoulder and calling my name. "Watson, Watson, get up, I have had a note from Hopkins, a policeman has been murdered in the very street where the ball of string was found yesterday. We are required in Canterbury. Dress quickly, there is a carriage waiting for us outside."

In a very few minutes we were in a carriage rushing through the empty streets of early morning London. Outside only the habitués of the great produce markets and a few revellers for whom the night had not yet finished were astir. Our carriage made good time and soon we were flying past Trafalgar Square. Even in the early hours of the morning Charing Cross impressed me with its air of being the very centre of the Empire, the point from which every road and track radiated outwards bearing its immense variety of goods and the trappings of power to every corner of the world.

We climbed into a mail train heading towards Canterbury West and Holmes slumped into the corner seat deep in thought. At last he said "Watson, you must see that I have blundered quite dreadfully and the price has been the life of a policeman, probably some young constable full of hope and enthusiasm for his work. What ever happens I will consider this case to be a personal failure."

"But Holmes," I protested, "you could not possibly have foreseen this tragedy."

"No, I am not a fortune teller, but if I had paid greater attention to this small detail I might well have warned Hopkins to give more care to the matter. The twine was extremely suggestive, but I failed to do exactly what I instructed Hopkins to do - follow the string."

"But what is it you see in this case. It is complete blackness to me at the moment," I replied.

"I see very little clearly, but I have a sense of where this is leading and I should perhaps have seen it last night."

"So what do we do?"

"As I said, we follow the string."

The scene of the murder was Kirby Lane, a small row of cottages just a couple of hundred yards from the West Station. They looked as if they had been thrown up in the recent past to accommodate the growing staff of the railway. They were mean and uninviting places of red brick, looking out onto a muddy lane where sewage and water mixed openly in small puddles. It was a prime example of the modern tendency to throw families into crowded conditions which are breeding grounds for disease and moral decline.

Hopkins emerged from a large crowd of constables, local residents and innumerable idle bystanders drawn by the excitement of the night's events. He looked drawn and dishevelled from lack of sleep. "Mr. Holmes, Dr. Watson, I am very grateful to you for coming down so swiftly. I hope you will excuse this call for assistance, but you appeared to read far more into that business of the ball of twine than I did and, as you see, it has now assumed much greater significance."

"I am very glad to be of service," replied Holmes. "I feel it is my duty to attempt to put right my blunder of yesterday. I should have devoted far more attention to that singular occurrence. But let us proceed to the matter. Outline the details if you would."

"As I understand it," began Hopkins, "Constable Martin, a young man of just twenty-two years, was walking his beat up St. Dunstan's Hill at about eleven o'clock last night. We cannot be sure, but he must have noticed something amiss down Kirby Lane and gone to investigate. The people living nearby say that they heard a shout as if of warning, and then some of them saw two men running out of the alley behind the houses. Martin, brave lad, tried to stop them and grappled one of them to the floor. In order to escape, the villain seems to have kicked at Martin's head mercilessly and one of those blows knocked the very life out of him. The body has been taken back to the police station. You may view it there if you feel it would be of help."

Holmes shook his head, I could see that his interest was already turning to the clues to be gathered from the immediate vicinity. "Have you followed my methods Hopkins?" he asked sharply. "What effort has been made to look for traces of the criminals?"

Hopkins gestured in a resigned fashion at the great throng of onlookers. "By the time I was alerted to the tragedy and had dispatched an officer to fetch you from Baker Street, the lane was already alive with every loafer in the city. I could not hope to find traces in such a maze of prints."

"Nonetheless," said Holmes, "we must look. Ask your constables to clear everyone out of the lane."

Hopkins knew that there was no arguing with my friend and set his men to the task with alacrity. It took all of five minutes to chase people into their houses or out onto the broader spaces of St. Dunstan's Hill. At last Holmes could set to his task. The local residents looked on in amazement as my colleague walked up and down the lane scouring every inch of ground.

For long minutes he disappeared into the alley behind the cottages and one or two of the bolder souls climbed up onto fences or walls in an attempt to watch Holmes at work. He emerged stooping low and peering at the ground like a bloodhound on the trail of a rabbit. Occasionally to the entertainment of his audience he would mutter pointedly to himself. As he reached the entrance to the lane from St. Dunstan's Hill he let out a cry of excitement and beckoned Hopkins and myself to join him.

ADVERTISEMENTS.

PATRONIZED BY H.R.H. THE PRINCE OF WALES, ETC., ETC.
J. CRAIK,
ARTISTIC PHOTOGRAPHER,
4, St. George's Gate, CANTERBURY
(OPPOSITE CATTLE MARKET).

Portraits of the Highest Excellence in all processes at Moderate Charges.
SPECIALITY IN FRAMED ENLARGEMENTS.
Every description of Outdoor Photography executed Promptly.
Established 1876.

FOR AFTERNOON TEAS & REFRESHMENTS,
SWEETS, ICES, FRUIT AND CREAM,
GO TO
TRAYTON BRAND'S,
ST. GEORGE'S GATE, CANTERBURY,
Opposite St. George's Terrace.

A pleasant walk of about 3 miles from Canterbury through fields.

Visitors provided with TEA and REFRESHMENTS at
CANTERBURY COTTAGE, LOWER HARDRES.

Furnished Apartments to Let, with attendance. Terms very Moderate. Good References.

If you are looking for a BUSINESS FURNISHED or UNFURNISHED HOUSES or APARTMENTS, please call or write—

MANAGER—
ROYAL DIAMOND COMMISSION AGENCY,
SUN STREET, CANTERBURY.

Auctioneers, Accountants, and General Trade Valuers.
Apartments and Houses for Cricket Week.

APARTMENTS, APARTMENTS, or BOARD RESIDENCE,

WARWICK HOUSE,
BEST LANE, CANTERBURY,
Close to Cathedral and Post Office.
Highly recommended. Perfect Sanitation.
Storage for Bicycles.

MRS. WRAIGHT,
Baker and Confectioner,
69, BURGATE STREET, CANTERBURY.

(On the direct route from the Cathedral to St. Augustine's College and St. Martin's Church).

Luncheons, Dinners, and Teas provided.

"Careful! Careful!" he cried. "You have already allowed virtually every mark of any value to be trampled under a dozen pairs of boots. But I have managed to isolate and follow a few marks from the alley to the end of the lane."

"You are a worker of miracles, Holmes," said Hopkins with genuine admiration. "What have you learnt?"

"Very little I am afraid. There were clearly two men, but that you already knew. They went down the alley as far as the back of the second house along, and then quickly turned and ran back the way they had come. I presume this was because they had been disturbed by your constable. I can see the signs of the struggle over there, and I can see the signs of two men fleeing again. As to their appearance all we can say with any certainty is that both men were of average height and, judging by the size of their boots, also of average build. They moved swiftly and without impediment, so we can assume they were in the prime of life. None of that, however, will mark them out from the majority of their fellow men. The problem is that most of the prints have been allowed to become very indistinct. I have only discovered this single, clear impression of one of their boots. I suggest you have one of your men make a sketch of this. It is a remarkably valuable print. I commend it to your attention."

Hopkins and I stared down at the mark, but it offered little to the untutored eye. Holmes, as impatient as ever, was already striding off towards the cottages, so Hopkins ordered a constable to preserve the precious imprint and hurried after my friend. We stopped in front of the second door in the row and Hopkins called out for widow Robbins to let us in.

She turned out to be one of those small, broad-hipped, grey haired women of the working classes who have carried many children, cared for a poorly paid husband, and is now left to eke out her days on a pitiful pension from the railway company. Although she was dressed in widow's weeds of sombre black from head to toe she appeared to be a bright and cheerful woman who was enjoying the drama that had erupted around her. Holmes turned his most winning persona on her and gently prompted her to give an account of the circumstances.

"Well, it's like this Mr. Holmes. I went out to fetch in the milk, as I have done every day since poor Mr. Robbins passed on, you see he used to fetch it home before then, and while I was out some ruffians broke the catch on my back window and jumped into the house."

"When was this?" asked Holmes.

"About eleven o'clock. I could hear the bells of St. Dunstan's chiming out the hour as I stepped onto the hill."

"Did you see anyone suspicious lurking around as you left?"

"No, I can't say as I did, but it's a busy place, what with the station and the carts going out to Whitstable and the like."

"And I understand that nothing was taken, is that right?"

"That's the strangest part, Mr. Holmes. All they did was to leave a ball of twine on the kitchen table and a couple of chairs out of place. It makes no sense to me, I can tell you."

"May I see the twine?" asked Holmes. The old woman reached up and took a battered tin biscuit box with a picture of the Queen on its lid, down off a high shelf. From within it she produced, like an ancient treasure, a tightly wound ball of heavy twine. Holmes took it and examined the ball minutely.

"As you suggested Hopkins, a very ordinary ball of twine. There are, you will note, two useful features. One is this gummed label which tells us that it was manufactured by Fox and Co. of Bermondsey. The other is that the twine has been cut, apparently with a rather blunt knife. It would be useful to know exactly how much was removed." Holmes tore the label off of the ball and handed it to me. The twine, he gave to Hopkins.

"Watson," he said in his usual commanding manner, "I want you to find out whether this could have been sold locally, and if so whether anyone recalls the sale. It is a long shot but worth the effort if you do not mind old fellow." I agreed without hesitation.

"Hopkins," he continued, "this ball of twine was twenty five yards long according to the label. I want you to ask one of your constables to measure it and tell me how much has been removed."

"What will you do Holmes?" I asked.

"I will follow the trail of that boot out there, which will take me directly to the local "House of Correction" as your prison proclaims itself."

"Why so?" asked Hopkins surprised.

"Because, my dear Inspector, the boot mark is of a cheap and unsatisfactory style commonly issued to convicts. Our murderers may recently have been resident in Canterbury Prison." We made to go, but Holmes paused to ask one last question. "How long have you lived here Mrs. Robbins?"

"Well," she said uncertainly as if the calculation might prove too taxing, "Mr. Robbins died three years ago this All Hallows and the company built them about three years prior to that. So six years in all, sir."

"Excellent, you have been an immense help in this matter. You were very wise to alert us to this strange business. I only wish that I had acted as swiftly." With that we left the blushing widow and went about our separate tasks agreeing to meet up in the nearby Falstaff Hotel at lunchtime.

As we left an old peddler passed us shuffling down the street. He was shabbily dressed wearing an old blanket for a shawl and, despite the hot weather, a battered cap for added warmth. As he shambled by he repeatedly cried:

"Pins, needles, cottons and thread
Boot laces, stay laces blacking and black lead."

On seeing the three of us he pushed his tray of cheap products towards us. Hopkins told him to be gone and he shuffled off up the hill still crying out in the same unconcerned manner, but I noticed Holmes staring after him for just a moment as if something about the peddler had caught his eye.

My morning was to prove disappointing. I had secured a directory listing local ironmongers, hardware and similar stores, but although all sold copious quantities of string and twine, none sold Fox and Co.'s products. At the last, I called into a large and well stocked store on the High Street. Behind the counter was a white haired old man who must have run the store since boyhood. He looked at the label and shook his head. "We used to stock this twine some years back, but Fox and Co. went out of business. Old man Fox died and there was no-one to carry on the trade. Good twine, mind you, but it is no longer sold anywhere to my knowledge."

I thanked him for the information and gave up the hunt, gladly returning to the bar of the Falstaff to await my companions in comfort.

By one o'clock the three of us were reunited around a table in a private dining room. A meal of local lamb and roasted potatoes was most welcome after the early start to the day. Hopkins had had a tiresome morning resolving the various details that the official police need to address in such a dreadful case. He had learnt, to Holmes' pleasure, that the missing length of string was seven feet. I told of my failure to find the merchant and of the apparent closure of the manufacturer.

"As I said," returned Holmes, "it was a very long shot. I am sorry your time has been so poorly used, but you had the compensation of a morning's stroll in the sunshine in beautiful surroundings."

I could tell by Holmes' demeanour that he was pleased with his morning's work and he needed no prompting to tell us about it. "Well gentlemen, our aim is to identify and capture the culprits for this heinous crime. I believe that I am able to tell you who they are, if not where they are." Hopkins and I both sat upright at this startling announcement. "Five days ago Joseph Patterson and Benjamin Potter were released from the local prison after serving six years for their central part in the Ramsgate jewel theft."

"Of course," cried Hopkins, "if ever a person should wear the title of blunderer it is me not you, Holmes. I should have foreseen this. They were bound to show their faces in the county."

"I am sorry, " I said, "but I am at a complete loss. Could you please explain what this is all about."

"A little over six years ago," Hopkins began, "a train passed by here carrying the Duc and Duchesse de Compiègnes to Ramsgate where they were to board a boat for the continent. The train was stopped at a signal and two men, Potter and Patterson, leapt on board. After threats of violence they made away with the Duchesse's jewel case. The men were picked up in Sevenoaks within a day, but the jewels were never recovered.

"I remember the case now that you mention it," I said. "But why should these men be interested in Kirby Lane?"

"Oh Watson!" exclaimed Holmes. "Is it really not clear?"

"Despite the name that the press gave to this attack," continued Hopkins with more patience, "it did not take place at Ramsgate. It occurred about four miles outside Canterbury on the Ramsgate line. It is very possible that Potter and his accomplice made their escape down the track and ended up in this vicinity."

"At which point," said Holmes, picking up the story in excitement, "they must have hidden the jewels. The most obvious hiding place was the building site where the new railway cottages were being thrown up."

"This is becoming clearer," I said. "But why the twine?"

"I cannot be certain," said Holmes "but my surmise is this. Patterson and Potter were both ill-educated thugs. Their literacy and numeracy are probably open to serious doubt. They may well have used the twine as a measuring device to pinpoint the place in which the jewels are concealed. It is quite a common device among the illiterate classes. I had already considered that as a possibility yesterday, which is why I asked Hopkins to determine how much twine was missing."

"You excel yourself Holmes," I said. "But how could two such ignorant men organise such a sophisticated crime?"

"An excellent question, Watson," he replied, "one which I think Hopkins can answer."

"Indeed, it has never been a secret that the two men were working for a third party, some kind of criminal mastermind. We have never, I must confess, even come close to laying a finger on him."

Silence descended on our small party as we pondered this new information. The landlord bustled in to clear the plates and offer further refreshment. After he had left, Holmes finally broke the thoughtful quiet. "We have two tasks gentlemen. One is to recover the jewels, the second is to lay our hands on the villains who perpetrated the murder of Martin as well as the mastermind behind both operations. Let us consider the first question for the moment."

"We must assume," said Hopkins picking up the thread, "that the gems are concealed in those cottages in Kirby Lane, do you not agree? The question is how we can retrieve them without the complete demolition of the cottages?"

Holmes replied immediately. "I believe that the problem can be resolved with the application of logic. We can take as our starting point the hypothesis that the jewels are in Widow Robbins' kitchen since the villains were devoting their attention to that room. We also know that a measurement of seven feet is involved, since that is the length of twine that had been removed from the ball. The question is from which point in the room and in which direction do we measure seven feet?"

"How can we know that without the assistance of those criminals?" I interjected.

"We cannot know for certain, but if we can reconstruct how far the building work had progressed on the night of the robbery, we might be able to identify a likely point. What do you think Hopkins?"

"It is worth considering. I will try and find the builder concerned and see if he can supply us with any record of the progress of the construction. I will send a message to you if I have any success." With that Hopkins left us to go about his task.

Just one hour later we received a note asking us to join Hopkins in Kirby Lane. We found him standing outside Widow Robbins' cottage deep in conversation with a stout red faced man. He was introduced to us as Arthur Tennant the owner of the firm that had built the houses. I must confess to having immediately taken against the man. He wore a bowler hat, waistcoat and shirt and a pair of grubby corduroy trousers. He gave the impression of spending as much time in the ale house as the building yard, and he smelled very strongly of alcohol.

For all that, as well as my prejudice against the shoddy construction of the houses, Tennant proved to be a most reliable informant. He carried a battered notebook which he consulted as Holmes questioned him. "I remember the day of that robbery very well. The men and me talked about nothing else over our bever in the morning break. Most of them would have fancied even a handful of the jewels in that box. No more digging and trowelling then. The houses were only just started, I would say that there was little more than the foundations down. Just imagine if we were sitting on the gems all the time. I reckon some of them would have kept those jewels if they'd found them."

"Can you say what the foundations looked like?" asked Holmes.

"I can do better than that," he searched through the pages of his book and then thrust it towards us. "There you are, that's an exact plan." The drawing was little more than a rough sketch surrounded by childish and ill-spelt instructions but it gave the definite shape of the foundations. "At that time, I reckon that we would just have had the basic shape of the houses down."

Holmes produced a folding measure from his pocket, extended it so that he had exactly seven feet and then calling us into the house, he set to work. "If I stand in the front parlour," he began, "the room is somewhat too long to take me into the kitchen from any of the corners that would have been visible to the men on that night. However, the kitchen itself is so small that I cannot measure out seven feet either way. I suggest, therefore, that the men started their measurement from the back left hand corner over which the stairs now mount. That would take us two feet and seven inches into the kitchen. My belief is that they would then have simply dug down in the earth and buried the jewels in the box, with the intention of reclaiming them very shortly."

"It is certainly worth trying," said Hopkins. "I will find a couple of constables to do the work for us."

While he was away, Holmes and I spoke to Widow Robbins who was only too pleased to allow a floorboard or two to be removed if it meant further celebrity for her little cottage. The constables were soon at work, gently easing the boards up. They lifted with depressingly little effort, revealing bare earth beneath. Holmes stepped forward and insisted on testing his hypothesis himself. Hopkins had brought a long metal pole which my colleague thrust down into the dirt. At his second attempt Holmes seemed to feel resistance. He knelt down and with a trowel provided by Tennant cleared the earth away. After only a matter of minutes, he stood up and turned towards us. In his hands was a mud encrusted box.

"Gentlemen, may I present the Duchesse de Compiègnes's gems." He lifted the lid and there, untouched by the filth in which they had lain was a glistening array of necklaces, pendants, rings and tiaras, such as one is rarely privileged to see. Holmes held them up item by item for his inspection and our admiration.

If Widow Robbins had had her way the jewels would have been paraded before all of her neighbours, but Holmes was insistent that the find should remain a well-kept secret in order to avoid alerting the criminals. Hopkins finally managed to prise the jewels from the old woman and dispatch them to a local bank for safe-keeping. Once the house had returned to a state of calm, I noticed that Holmes had lapsed into contemplation, pulling out his pipe, stuffing it with tobacco and using it as an aid to thought as he had so many times before. Hopkins and I knew better than to interrupt him at these moments. We sat drawing on our own pipes until the room was a thick fug of smoke.

"These deductions and discoveries are all very satisfying, but they bring us no closer to finding the men," was all he would say for over half an hour.

"There is no alternative," he said at last. "The men must come back. They will not desert their spoil, we must watch in the hope of picking them out." Thus it was arranged that Holmes and I would spend the rest of the afternoon watching the movement of people up and down Kirby Lane. Our vantage point was to be Widow Robbins' own bedroom, which she gladly allowed us to use.

It was a small, whitewashed room with little furniture beyond a bed, a table with a water jug and a battered tin box which presumably contained her entire wardrobe. The room was well kept but water was clearly leaking into the house whenever it rained. There were two brown stains down either side of the window and the whole room stank of damp, testaments to the shoddy workmanship used in building such dwellings.

Holmes and I sat back from the window and waited. It was arranged that Widow Robbins would be on hand to identify local people if necessary. The wait was to be long and tedious. The old woman readily identified most of the visitors to the lane. Fishmongers, butchers, bakers, all passed by as they did most every day. Occasional strangers all seemed to have legitimate business with one or other of the neighbouring houses.

As seven o'clock approached, Holmes tapped me on the shoulder and suggested I fetch Hopkins from the police station and bring him back to discuss our course of action. As I prepared to leave I glanced down into the street and saw the old peddler that Hopkins had turned away that morning. "I have never seen him before," said the old widow behind us.

"He was here first thing this morning," I protested.

"Well, I have never seen him down this way before now," she insisted.

"A possibility!" cried Holmes, rubbing his hands together in excitement. "A most definite possibility."

"He seems too small and feeble," I suggested.

"You forget yourself Watson," my friend replied. "Have you not seen me dressed in such a guise. This man is at least six feet tall, but he has mastered the peddler's burdened stoop to perfection."

"I grant you his height, but he is too thin to have been a match for poor Martin," I continued.

"If I am right, we are not looking at one of the two thugs, but rather the mastermind himself. If this is genuine disguise, it shows a cunning and a daring beyond Patterson and Potter. I must say that this fellow caught my attention this morning. He possesses a singular, but almost imperceptible, characteristic which I noticed earlier."

I knew better than to seek an explanation of my friend's cryptic remark, instead I asked "Shall I challenge him Holmes?"

"Ever the man of action, Watson," said my friend with a laugh. "No, we must try and take the whole gang. After all this fellow is not the murderer. We must wait our moment and then set out on his trail like bloodhounds."

"You mean follow him?"

"Exactly. Are you with me?"

"Of course," I replied.

We descended the rickety uncarpeted stairs and watched the shabby fellow from the window of the tiny parlour. He strolled up and down the lane several times crying his wares all the while, like the genuine article. As he shambled along, however, it was obvious that he was glancing from side to side. Our suspicions were strengthened when he slipped down the alley behind the cottages. That gave Holmes the opportunity to leave the house and make for the end of the lane where he could conceal himself. I would follow on at a further distance behind.

The peddler re-emerged from the alley and wandered slowly back down the lane. He called out his wares as he went and continually thrust his tray of laces and polish in front of every passer-by. He was so convincing a hawker that I began to doubt the accuracy of Holmes' identification.

I watched as the peddler turned down St. Dunstan's Hill towards the city centre, followed at a discernible distance by Holmes. I lingered for a few moments and then joined the pursuit. There was no difficulty in keeping the shabby figure in view. He walked very slowly, occasionally stopping and even selling an item or two from his tiny stock. His ragged dress marked him out from the citizens of this prosperous city.

He shambled through the Westgate and turned immediately down into Pound Lane which ran behind the old walls towards the northern side of the city. This was a much quieter route than the High Street and suggested that our quarry was not as eager to peddle his wares as his earlier demeanour had indicated. The lack of people also made it much harder to keep our pursuit secret. We crossed the river and found ourselves in a maze of backstreets, in which we continually lost sight of the peddler as he turned corners ahead of us. I had joined Holmes by this time and we were walking side by side, trying to look like visitors admiring the quieter quarters of the city.

"I fear he may have sensed our presence now," murmured Holmes. "He glanced back a few moments ago as he turned a corner. He may try and lose us in these narrow lanes." In truth, he did the exact opposite, but it proved equally effective in its own way.

As we turned yet another corner, our fears were realised. The peddler was nowhere to be seen. Two or three alleys turned off on either side and Holmes dashed forward to catch a glimpse of the fleeing figure. To our surprise the man had not disappeared. He was standing just around a corner, calmly packing his grimy clay pipe with shag.

"Could I trouble either of you gentlemen for a light? he asked in a wheezy, grating voice. Holmes handed him a box of vestas and stood regarding him as he lit his pipe.

"Much obliged," he said handing back the matches. "Can I interest you in any laces, shoe black, or the like?" Holmes bent over the tray and picked through its contents, looking at each item with some care and engaging in idle chatter before buying a pair of black laces. Once the purchase had been made, the peddler persisted cleverly in showing no sign of pursuing his journey. Holmes and I were, thereby, compelled to move on.

"We have a foe worthy of the name today," said Holmes as we walked back towards the cathedral. "I am glad to say, however, that he has given us one clue which, I believe will help bring him to justice. A clue, I must add, that I have been too blind to see, despite literally holding it in my hands. He has also confirmed something that I suspected this morning, a suspicion which adds an intriguing twist to this tale."

"Could we not simply have laid hands on him there and then?" I asked.

"On what evidence?" Holmes rightly pointed out. "Moreover we are here to catch a murderer as well as a jewel thief. I want him to lead us to his partners in crime."

"So how will you find him?" I asked.

"You will show me the way, Watson."

"What do you mean? I have no more idea of their whereabouts than you do. How can I help?"

"You told me that one of the merchants you visited this morning had known Fox and Co. I want you to take me to him."

ADVERTISEMENTS.

BAKER'S
Commercial Temperance Hotel
AND
RESTAURANT,
St. George's Street, Canterbury,
(Main Street, Facing the Corn Exchange).

Established 1874.

ONE MINUTE FROM POST OFFICE AND CATHEDRAL.
BUS FROM EITHER STATION 6D.

Hot Joints from 12 to 3.   Large Cycle Store.

QUIET, CENTRAL, AND HOMELY.   BATH ROOM.
ELECTRIC LIGHT THROUGHOUT.
A. G. BAKER, Proprietor.

When you refer to your GUIDE BOOK for PLACES of INTEREST, please notice

E. GEESON'S,
THE CASH TAILOR,
44, Burgate Street,
(Corner of Butchery Lane).

Points of interest to you will be:—

His low Prices.—Suit from 30/-.
His execution of Orders.—Two clear days if required.
His Fit and Cut.—Faultless.

A TRIAL ORDER WILL CONVINCE YOU.

"Gladly Holmes, but why?"

He reached into his pocket and pulled out the laces that he had just bought. "This is the reason," he said handing them to me. I stared at them blankly but I knew it was pointless asking Holmes to explain his chain of reasoning any further, so I fell in beside him and showed him the way to the hardware store in the High Street.

The old shopkeeper was still at his post behind the counter. It was quite possible to believe that he had remained there day in and day out for the last fifty years. "Good afternoon sir," he said to me. "Can I be of some further assistance to you?"

"Thank you," I replied, "but it is my colleague here who wishes to ask you some questions."

The merchant gave a slight nod in Holmes' direction and listened attentively as he spoke. "My friend, Dr. Watson, has told me that you recall a firm by the name of Fox and Co. who ceased trading some years ago."

"I do indeed sir. They sold a first class selection of strings and other household goods."

"Including shoelaces?" asked Holmes looking in my direction.

"I believe so," said the old man.

"Do you happen to recall whether there was a particular merchant locally who acted as their agent?"

The merchant hesitated for only a moment before replying. "Hartson and Rice used to act as their agent. But they have also ceased trading. Old Hartson died three years back and Mr. Rice decided to retire to his farm outside Dover."

"Where did they hold their stock?" asked Holmes, as I began to dimly perceive the trail that my colleague was pursuing. The old man reached under his counter and retrieved a huge maroon ledger which he needed both hands to haul onto the surface. He opened it with the respect due to a worthy tome and turned through several pages before alighting on a particular entry.

"Here you are, sir," he said turning the volume in our direction. "Darenth Yard. You will find that it is about half a mile out of the city on the road to Fordwich. It is a collection of old wooden sheds where a number of merchants have space to store their stock. I think the Hartson and Rice storeroom is still untenanted."

"Come Watson. We have no time to lose," said Holmes urgently. He turned to the merchant and thanked him energetically. "I am confident that the information that you have given me will be of the greatest value in bringing the perpetrators of a most heinous crime to justice. I am most grateful for your help."

We left the old man looking confused and bewildered as Holmes rushed out of the store. "Do you see how this information is the key to their whereabouts Watson?" he asked.

"I am beginning to grasp your train of thought," I replied uncertainly.

"Your excellent work this morning supplied me with the clue. The link is, of course, the products manufactured by Fox and Co. How is it that this peddler has a copious supply of goods produced by a company that foundered some years ago? Where did the burglars find the ball of string produced by the same company? We know, as you discovered, that they could not have purchased these goods locally, and it seems unlikely that even if they were available elsewhere in the country, that the brains behind this affair would decide to bring such a supply with him. Yet, in his tray, our peddler had a number of Fox and Co. products. More to the point, if you look at the laces that I gave you what do you notice?"

I pulled the items from my pocket and examined them. "They are somewhat dirty," I replied.

"Indeed they are, and if you look at the paper sleeve you will notice a number of little brown damp stains. When I put them to my nose there was a definite musty smell. Clearly these products have been lying around in a store unused for several years. Does it not seem likely that such a location would also make an ideal hiding place for two newly released felons and their master?"

"That is a positive master stroke, Holmes," I said. In all the years I worked with that brilliant mind, I never lost my admiration for those moments of lucidity which he brought to the most complex problems. "But can you be sure that Hartson and Rice are the only company with stores of this kind?"

"The hour is getting late, we must play this card while we have the chance and see what it brings us," said my colleague with resolution as we walked briskly down the High Street. "We need to act quickly and examine the possibility that the three criminals are concealed in Darenth Yard. I will head there immediately. You must find Hopkins and persuade him to bring men, and preferably armed men, to meet me there."

I nodded my assent and was about to take my leave when Holmes called me back. "Whatever you do, approach with great caution. These are most dangerous men. I do not want to lose the element of surprise."

Holmes' name carried great weight with Stanley Hopkins and the briefest explanation of the situation was sufficient for him to spring into action. He gathered eight constables and pocketed one of a pair of revolvers while handing its counterpart to me. "Holmes is right to be cautious. I fear these men will turn out to be vicious if cornered."

We all climbed into two police carriages and swung out of the yard onto the road heading out towards Fordwich. The few minutes between my arrival at the station and our departure had seen the onset of dusk. Lights were beginning to show in the windows of the shops and houses and red lamps swayed on the carriages ahead of us. I recall very clearly sensing that attempting to restrain such men under cover of darkness would bring real peril, but I could never have guessed how accurate that prediction would prove to be.

The road was in poor condition so we bounced and swayed as the driver urged on the horses. What with the dark and the attention we were having to pay to holding on to our seats, I almost missed the figure of Holmes flagging us down by the side of the road, but at the last moment he caught my attention and I banged on the roof for the driver to stop.

"The yard is just down there," he said gesturing towards an entrance between two rotting wooden fences. "There are definitely signs of life but as yet I can not identify how many people are in there or who they might be."

"What do you want us to do?" asked Hopkins.

"I suggest that you detail your men around the perimeter of the yard while I approach the warehouse and discover who is in there."

"I will not allow you to go alone," I said. "I have a revolver and you should not approach them without such cover."

"Your concern is unnecessary, Watson, but I know from long experience that you will not allow me to go alone, so I will not argue. I insist only on absolute quiet from all concerned."

We watched the constables moving into their positions around the yard and then Holmes touched me on the arm and we began to move forward. The entrance between the fences had a board listing the companies who worked within. Hartson and Rice were named, but the paint was now peeling and faded suggesting long years of abandonment. The gateway gave onto a muddy yard about the size of a rugby pitch. This was filled with carts and barrows of all kinds for moving the produce stored in the sheds that surrounded the yard on three sides.

"The third one on the left is the old Hartson and Rice shed," whispered Holmes. The sun had now set and it would have been impossible to determine which storehouse was which, if it had not been for the signs of a light coming from the upper floor of one of the buildings. We stole quietly forward, keeping close to the line of the warehouses. The store could only be entered by either a pair of large double doors which appeared to be padlocked and bolted or the small entrance inset into these doors.

We stopped by the doors and listened intently. At first there were only the normal night sounds, traffic moving on the road outside, bats fluttering and the far off sound of church bells. After a minute or so, I began to discern movements within, feet shuffling and what sounded like pots being moved around. Holmes turned and nodded that he had heard and pointed to the small door. We approached and Holmes gave it a gentle push. To my surprise it swung open almost silently. We waited for a moment and then Holmes and I peered round into the interior of the store.

There was nothing to be seen on the darkened ground floor other than large piles of straw strewn here and there, but a wooden staircase led up to another level on which a light was clearly visible. Holmes pulled me back and we moved away from the door. "We will need all the constables in order that we may enter in force. You and I could not overpower these men alone. Go back to Hopkins, Watson, and bring the men over here. But remember, we must move in absolute silence. I will wait here."

Hopkins called his men together and we moved towards the store, but our venture was doomed to end in disaster. As we crossed the yard a tall, gangly, young constable in the middle of the group tripped and crashed into a pile of paint tins. The sound echoed around the yard and we knew that it was impossible for the villains not to have heard us.

There were shouts and curses within the building and I saw a figure appear at the door, who seeing the constables, slammed it shut and dropped a bar into place behind it. Hopkins immediately took control of the situation, shouting out a warning to the people inside that they should immediately surrender. The reply was instant and deadly. Two or three shots rang out from both the ground floor and upper levels. In the darkness they flew wide of their mark, but sent all of us falling flat on to our stomachs. When we looked up the flames were just beginning to catch.

It was obvious that one of the shots must have caught something within the store and flames were licking at the door frame. There were shouts and movement all around. Hopkins barked orders for his constables to seek water, and there were cries as they stumbled about. These mingled with desperate shouts and ghastly noises which emanated from the store.

I expected the door to fly open at any moment and three figures to burst out. It never happened. The fire must have devoured the wood and straw in moments. Within a minute of the shot the front of the store was a sheet of flame, and five minutes later the whole yard was ablaze at who knows what cost to the merchants of Canterbury. At the last, when it seemed that no-one could have survived, the goods entrance on the first floor swung open. A tall figure was momentarily silhouetted against the flames, and then with an agonising scream tumbled to the ground twenty feet below.

I rushed towards the broken figure and found him still to be breathing but barely sensible. I did what little I could for him, but he died as he lay there, whether from the flames or the fall, I could not tell. Holmes craned over me and stared down at the lifeless body. "Our peddler, I believe," he said simply and then returned to battle with the all-devouring flames.

We spent a dismal night helping the constables and the local fire brigade to douse the fire. It was a nigh on impossible task given the dry conditions and the combustible timber and merchandise lying all around. By dawn there was little more for us to do. Towards dawn, Hopkins rubbed the dirt and soot from his hands and said "I assume that is the end of the strange business of the ball of twine. I only wish it had had a more satisfactory conclusion. I have no doubt that the perpetrators were punished, but I would not wish such a vile end on even the most evil of men. I am sure, Holmes, that you would have found it satisfying to learn the identity of the mastermind of this event."

"His would certainly be a name worth including in my index, but I am not despairing of identifying him yet. If you would both meet me at Baker Street this evening, I may be able to shed some further light on this matter." Holmes made to leave us and then turned back. "I would be grateful if you could bring at least one of the jewels from the box with you as well Hopkins."

With that he disappeared from the scene, leaving me to clean myself up at the police station and then return to London for a well-deserved afternoon of sleep. Hopkins arrived at about eight o'clock that evening, closely followed by Holmes who seemed flushed with excitement.

"Yesterday, gentlemen, we set ourselves two tasks, one was to identify the culprits in this affair, the second was to apprehend them," Holmes began in his usual logical manner. "We have, in the most tragic of manners, laid hands on the villains. We also know the identity of two of them, thus one question remains 'who is the third person in this case?'"

"I assume that he was the peddler, but what clue can we have to his identity?" I asked.

"We have two clues. The first is very simple, when I heard the peddler speak I caught the faintest intonation in his voice. Although he spoke the most colloquial of English, I could still detect the gentle rolling of the letter 'r' as he spoke. I was certain that this man was a native French speaker.

That clue could serve to make matters more rather than less difficult. It would be hard enough to identify an English criminal let alone a French one. However, I was supplied with one further clue. Hopkins, do you have the jewel I asked you to bring?"

Hopkins handed him a white handkerchief. My friend unwrapped the small bundle and revealed a brilliant diamond that I recognised as one of those that we had rescued from Kirby Lane. Holmes handed it to me and said "Take a good look at it Watson."

I picked up the stone and held it up to the light. Then I stood and walked over to his desk and examined the diamond through a lens.

"This stone is paste," I said to Holmes without any trace of doubt. "Were all the stones the same?"

"I believe so," said Holmes.

Hopkins was astounded. He took the gem from me and examined it himself from every possible angle. At last he laid it to one side and said "This is a very bitter harvest," he said. "It seems wrong that a young policeman and three criminals should die for a handful of worthless stones." He paused for a moment and then returned to the investigation. "I fail to see where this takes us. This only serves to deepen the mystery."

"Possibly," said Holmes, "but, on the other hand, it offered one possibility that I felt was worth exploring. It was possible, I decided, that if they were fake, the owners of the jewels may have had a vested interest in their theft. I decided to see if the Duc de Compiègnes matched the description of our down at heel peddler. This is the result."

He handed us a cutting from a society magazine. I unfolded it and there was a sketch of a man who was recognisably the corpse I had held in my arms last night. "This is astonishing, Holmes," I said. "What do you make of it?"

"I have no doubt that the Duc and possibly the Duchesse had either sold their stones for cash or were hoping to claim some insurance on them. Whichever was the case, it was in their interests to have the stones disappear. Thus a robbery was arranged, which would presumably have resulted in the Duc reclaiming the stones from the robbers in exchange for a small fee, in order to avoid the embarrassment of recognisably fake gems appearing in the hands of reputable jewellers. Unfortunately, the plan failed and both parties had to wait six years for its conclusion. It was a dangerous game and one which ultimately cost the Duc his life."

"This is a scandal of the highest order," I exclaimed.

"Very true Doctor," said Hopkins, "but, I wager that it is not one that my superiors will ever allow me to investigate." We all lapsed into a long and contemplative silence.
"An inglorious end to an inglorious case," said Holmes as he rose and bid us both goodnight.